On principle, Gisele disliked and dis-
trusted everything about Nathaniel
Oakley; he was just the kind of man
who had caused her so much heart-
searching in the past. But then she
found herself having to pose as his
fiancée. Thrown so intimately into his
company, would even Gisele be able to
resist him?

IMPULSIVE CHALLENGE

BY

MARGARET MAYO

MILLS & BOON LIMITED
15–16 BROOK'S MEWS
LONDON W1A 1DR

First published in Great Britain 1986 by Mills & Boon Limited

© Margaret Mayo 1986

Australian copyright 1986 Philippine copyright 1986 This edition 1986

ISBN 0 263 75355 7

Set in Monophoto Plantin 10 on 11 pt. 01–0586 – 54746

Printed and bound in Great Britain by Collins, Glasgow

CHAPTER ONE

NATHANIEL OAKLEY was a typical example of the arrogant male Gisele hated. He had taken over Thorne & Forest Advertising when it was on the verge of being put in the hands of the receivers. He stalked the corridors like a predatory tiger, and it was heaven help anyone he caught not doing their job.

Most of the girls had already fallen head over heels in love with him. Gisele heard tales of a voice that was deep and sensual, a body like a Greek god and dark mysterious eyes that could melt you on the spot.

Outside in the car park his silver Porsche made the other cars look like heaps of junk. It had an ostentatious red flash along each side and bore the personalised registration, NO I. Number One in everything he did, whether it was running a business or conducting his private affairs.

It was common knowledge that girls fell like ninepins at his feet. That he had merely to lift a finger and they were his to do with as he liked—and then he discarded them, like Adrian had her!

He was so representative of the man she hated that Gisele felt sick each time she thought about him, and grew tired of listening to everyone singing his praises.

'Men like him need taking down a peg or two,' she said to Ruth in the typing pool one day, 'not have their disgusting male egos boosted further by every girl they meet drooling over them!'

'How can you resist him?' Ruth rolled her eyes expressively. 'He's the dishiest man I've ever seen. What wouldn't I give for a date with him!'

'Me too,' said Sally and Helen in unison, looking equally besotted.

'Well, I think you're mad, the lot of you,' returned Gisele bitterly. 'All you'd end up with is heartache.'

'Just because you've had one fatal affair it doesn't mean all men are the same,' protested Ruth.

Gisele eyed her angrily. 'I bet *he* is. He's the love 'em and leave 'em type.' Or at least that was the impression she had gained. She had never actually spoken to him or even seen him, but she did not need to; she had heard enough to convince her.

In bed that night Gisele cast her mind back over the events that had made her wary of men. It began when her father died and her mother remarried. Her own father had been loving, kind, gentle, fun to be with. Her stepfather was violent-tempered and often brutal.

From the age of twelve to eighteen she had seen her mother reduced from a handsome, intelligent woman to a nervous wreck. It had taught her to despise the type of man her stepfather was.

To look at him no one would have guessed at the monster lurking within. He was a good-looking man with a fine body and a quick wit. Most people liked James. Her mother had been taken in completely by his charming manner and ready tongue.

It was not until he had installed himself in their home that her mother had discovered his true character—the sharp flare of temper, his selfishness, his greed for money, his weakness for other women, and his resentment of her love for her pretty daughter.

Her mother had been relatively well off. Over the years she had accumulated quite a nest-egg, and that, together with her husband's life insurance, amounted to a considerable sum.

James had not been slow to take advantage, arranging holidays abroad her mother did not really want, but which she went along with to keep the peace, buying a new car, spending more and more money on drink, and generally having a good time.

He lost his job through bad time-keeping, and his anger against her mother, when she tried to reason with him, turned into physical violence.

For as long as she could she stuck it, but in the end could bear it no longer. Gisele woke one morning to discover she had taken an overdose.

Even after all this time she ached thinking about it. Her fingers curled beneath the sheets and hot tears burnt the back of her eyes. It was an experience she never wanted to go through again.

She had left home and her first flat here, in London, had been at the top of a tenement building where she looked out at chimneypots and roofs and very little else.

It had been shabby and poky and a complete contrast to what she was used to, but it had also been the beginning of a new life, a challenge, and she had managed to find a job in the typing pool of Thorne & Forest Advertising.

Not that she intended remaining a copy typist all her life; she was not wasting two years' secretarial training. It was her ambition to become personal assistant to some top-notch business executive. But jobs were not that easy when you were inexperienced, so she settled for being a typist until she was ready for something better.

And then she met Adrian! It did not upset her thinking about Adrian; it made her angry. She clenched her fists as she recalled how he had swept her off her feet. She had been bowled over by his Nordic good looks. His blue eyes had melted her bones and she had fallen immediately in love, never dreaming that she was really looking for someone to fill the gap after her mother's death.

Adrian was the wealthy son of a merchant banker, keen to follow in his father's footsteps. Gisele had literally bumped into him in the National Gallery one lunchtime. He had apologised profusely for not looking where he was going and promptly invited her out to dinner that evening.

It had been a whirlwind affair, and in no time at all they were engaged and their forthcoming wedding announced in *The Times*.

His parents, unfortunately, had been less keen— barely polite, making it clear they thought Adrian was making a big mistake, and all the time harping on some other girl they clearly thought he should marry.

But Gisele had no doubt at all in her own mind. She loved Adrian with every fibre of her being. That he was less emotional did not strike her as odd. He had asked her to marry him, that was enough.

On the morning of the wedding, unable to sleep, she was up at the break of dawn, and found a letter pushed through her letterbox. Every single word was imprinted in her memory for all time.

Gisele, *it said*,

I know this will come as a shock and I'm being a coward for writing instead of telling you myself—but I can't go through with it. I never really intended things to go this far.

The truth is, I love someone else. We'd had one hell of a row before I met you and she'd sworn she never wanted to see me again.

I felt sure, though, that she still loved me and decided the only way to get her back was to make her jealous. She came to see me today—I'd almost given up hope—and begged me not to go through with the wedding.

You're so sweet, Gisele, you don't deserve any of this. I've used you unashamedly and I truly am sorry.

If it's any consolation I don't think much of myself either. Please find it in your heart to forgive me—I was desperate.

Adrian

The nerve of the man! He had even enclosed a cheque for a thousand pounds. Never had Gisele felt so humiliated in her life. How dared he do this to her! How dared he use her in this manner! He and James were two of a pair. Why hadn't she learned by her mother's mistake?

But it had taught her a lesson. Never again would she let any man near. They were swine, all of them. They used women for their own ends, with no heed at all for feelings that got devastated in the process.

No wonder he had made a big issue out of announcing their marriage! It had all been part of his carefully calculated plan to get his girl back.

She tore the cheque into shreds and posted it to him, wondering what would have happened if his girl hadn't turned up at the crucial moment. Would she have had the big rejection in any case? She guessed so. What a fool she had been; what a gullible, naïve fool!

But despite Gisele's carefully assumed icy exterior she was never short of invitations. Ruth told her it was her red-gold hair and wide jewel-green eyes that made men take a second glance. Someone else told her it was because of her model-girl figure.

Gisele did not think she was all that stunning. Admittedly her eyes were bright and clear, her skin smooth, but she was too tall, too thin, to be a raving beauty.

And her hair, her untameable red hair, was the bane of her life. Its deep waves went any way except the one she wanted them to go. How she longed for sleek straight hair that would look chic, that could be coaxed into any number of styles.

But men, unfortunately, seemed drawn to her like bees round honey. Not a week went by when someone did not invite her out—and always she rejected them. She was finished with men—for all time.

She had heard through the grapevine that Adrian was now married, so at least he had achieved his object—even though he had broken her heart in the process. She could not understand how any man could use a woman for purely selfish reasons. It sickened her, it really did.

Her promotion from the typing pool to secretary to Bill Spalding, the Creative Director, was a step in the right direction so far as her career was concerned. And with the resultant rise in salary she was able to move out of her shoddy flat into brighter and better-furnished rooms, where she added a few bits and pieces of her own so that it gradually became a home, a haven where she could relax and be herself.

Her career was all that mattered. She might even go one step further than the personal assistant she had promised herself and become an advertising executive instead. An equal to Nathaniel Oakley! Wouldn't that be satisfying?

It came as a shock a few days later when she was summoned to his office. She could not imagine why he wanted to see her; she was not even aware that he knew of her existence.

Miles of corridor seemed to separate her own office from his. His suite was two storeys up and she ignored the lift, using the stairs, trying to delay the moment when she met this notoriously virile male specimen.

Outside the heavy oak door she paused to pat her hair into some semblance of order, hoping it would not let her down. She wanted to appear calm and cool, even though she felt on edge. It was not every day one was called to the executive suite.

It came as no surprise to discover that his secretary was a pretty blonde with pouting lips and a voluptuous figure. The girl glanced disdainfully at Gisele. 'Miss Latham? Mr Oakley's on the telephone, you can sit there,' nodding towards a chair near a door which Gisele assumed led into his office. 'He shouldn't be long.'

Her attitude did not invite questions, even though Gisele would have liked to ask about the man who wanted to see her. She could hear his voice, deep and resonant—a rich voice, a sexy voice. The girls were right in that respect at least.

Even listening to it through the door, unable to hear exactly what he was saying, was enough to make Gisele realise what an attractive voice it was—the sort you could listen to and become hypnotised. A voice that sent strange tingles through your limbs so that you strained to hear each word, listened to the inflections that gave it its appeal. The deep timbre must have set many a woman's heart fluttering. It was a distinctive voice, one not easily forgotten.

And then the door opened. Even before she looked across Gisele became aware of a man of strength, of great power. It emanated from him like warmth from a fire. 'Come in, Miss Latham.' The command boomed from somewhere deep in his throat.

She lifted the thick lashes that framed her lustrous green eyes, turning her head to look at him, accentuating the slim column of her throat, the proud upward thrust of her breasts. She resented the imperious way he spoke, but had no intention at this stage of revealing her annoyance.

Instead she smiled, her generous lips parting to reveal even white teeth. Unconsciously she lifted a hand and smoothed her unruly hair, then with one fluid movement she rose.

Gisele had a natural, unconscious grace. She did not even know that her actions could be misconstrued, that any man, or woman for that matter, could think she was deliberately using her body to draw attention to herself.

But she did note that Nathaniel Oakley's jet-black brows drew into a straight line and wondered what she had done to annoy him. It was no more than a passing thought, however, for she became immediately aware of the magnetism every girl on the company was talking about.

Never had she met a man so compellingly male. Gisele was tall, but he towered above her, broad-shouldered, slim-hipped, and devastating! It was impossible to drag her eyes away.

Even when he turned back into his office she was left with the impression of a pair of piercing dark eyes that could see into your very soul, of a long straight nose, lips that were at this moment grim but could be extremely sensual, a harsh square jaw, and above all an overpowering arrogance.

He had a long, loose-limbed stride that took him across the room so quickly that she was still in the doorway when he turned. Again she felt the impact of those deep dark eyes.

It stopped her in her tracks so that for a second she did nothing more than look at him. A blue shirt, unbuttoned at the collar, rolled up to his elbows, emphasised the width of shoulder and did little to hide the powerful chest. Pale grey trousers outlined his muscular thighs and drew attention to their long rangy length.

The jacket to his suit was flung carelessly over the back of a chair, as was his tie. He looked like a man of action, a man used to hard work and not afraid of getting down to it. Somehow it did not go with the image Gisele had of a womaniser.

'I trust you're not going to stand there all day?' The cold sarcasm goaded her into action. She blinked, as though snapping out of a dream, and walked forward into the room.

He watched her closely, insolently, studying her from head to toe. She might almost have been naked instead of in a neat navy skirt and spotted blouse. They showed off to perfection her long legs and slim hips, the enticing curve of her breasts and her slender throat. But they were not intended that way. Gisele did not dress to appeal to the opposite sex, she dressed to please herself.

But observing the way Nathaniel Oakley's eyes raked over her she felt sure he thought she was deliberately being provocative, and was appalled to discover that this appraisal sent her pulses racing and her nerve-ends tingling.

She halted in front of his desk. They stood facing each other for what seemed like minutes, but could have been no more that a couple of seconds. His eyes held hers. They were like bottomless pits, deep and dark and quite unfathomable. It was impossible to read what was going through his mind.

Gisele felt a strange quiver run through each and every limb until she shook like a jelly. With an effort she dragged her eyes away. At the same time he reached out and touched her hair, a touch so light she would not have known had she not seen him do it.

'Beautiful, quite beautiful,' he growled huskily.

She tossed her head, doing her best to ignore the sudden warmth she had felt from that lean-fingered hand—an awareness, a warning that he was an extremely dangerous male animal. 'I can't believe you asked me here to discuss my hair!'

He smiled, a lazy smile that lit up his eyes from within and lifted the corners of his lips. The harsh arrogance disappeared, though Gisele was not sure for how long, and he beckoned her to sit.

'You're right, that was not my reason. It's quite remarkable, though, like a halo of fire. Have you a temper to match?'

Gesele felt she was being deliberately baited and eyed him warily as she took the indicated seat, crossing her slim ankles, folding her hands demurely in her lap and refusing to answer.

She expected him to sit too, but instead he walked round to her side of the desk and leaned back against it. His smile did not look entirely sincere. He was playing some game she could not quite fathom.

When he again allowed his eyes to slide over her body, lingering where the vee of her blouse very discreetly revealed the suggestion of a curve, she decided she was being weighed up.

'If you've quite finished,' she said tightly, 'perhaps we might get on with the business of why I'm here.'

'In good time, Miss Latham. In good time.'

'I do have work to do,' she said irately, flashing her green eyes and wishing he had not the power to make her feel quite so uncomfortable. She felt sure he had X-ray eyes, that he could see through her clothes to her body beneath, and was deriving a great deal of satisfaction from his examination. 'And I'm sure you're a busy man too.'

He folded his arms across his tightly muscled chest. 'Indeed I am, but never too busy to look at a pretty woman.'

Gisele swallowed hastily. Lord, he was at it already! She had heard he was a fast worker, but this was ridiculous. She tried to look at him, intending to put him in his place with a scornful glance. Instead she found her gaze sliding away from his smiling face to fix themselves on his arms—somewhere safe!

Bulging biceps strained against the rolled shirt-sleeves, sinewy forearms were covered with dark silky hairs, and his hands were lean and well-shaped. She found herself wondering what it would be like to be held by those strong arms, to feel those pliant hands caressing her body. Then she shook her head and mentally berated herself for harbouring such thoughts.

She lifted her eyes once again to his face. He was watching her, and she had the uneasy feeling that he knew exactly what thoughts were going through her mind. He looked amused and confident as he moved round to take his seat at the other side of the desk.

Relief washed over Gisele. At last there was some solid object between them! But if she thought this would make her immune to his virility she was mistaken.

He raked a hand through his thick black hair, pushing back his seat and swivelling disconcertingly, his eyes never once leaving her face. 'How long have you worked for this company?'

'Three years,' she replied, wishing he would keep still. He was making her dizzy with his constant movement. Or was it the effect of those penetrating eyes, or those sensual lips, or the tough jutting line of his jaw?

He was a proud man, a noble man, and he was fully aware of the impact he was having on her. Was he like this with all women? she wondered. Did he reduce them to a state of jittering nerves before he moved in to make his kill?

'So that makes you—how old?' He stopped and rested his elbows on the desk, his chin on his hands.

'It's in the company records,' she said sharply before she could stop herself. 'Why don't you check up if it's so important?'

'I have,' he returned coolly. 'Twenty-one, is that correct? Twenty-two in December.'

'In that case why did you bother to ask?' she demanded, then remembered he was the boss and she a mere employee. 'I'm sorry, I shouldn't have spoken like that—it was very rude. Do forgive me.'

His lips quirked. 'My guess was right. The lady does have a temper.'

'From my Irish grandmother,' she said crossly, long lashes fluttering over her expressive eyes.

'God bless the Irish,' he said irreverently. 'I like a woman with spirit.'

'And I wish you'd get to the point.' Gisele made a show of looking at her watch. 'Mr Spalding will wonder where I am.'

'Bill knows you're with me.'

Did he also know that the new head of the company was a woman-eater? That it was doubtful many of them got out of here alive? And the blonde out there, was she listening with her ear to the door? Was she eaten up with jealousy because another woman was closeted with her boss? Or was she immune to his charm? Did she perform her duties stoically, ignoring the sexy male predator that he was?

It was hardly likely. He was attractive to women—and what was more damning, he knew it! He was enjoying himself now, enjoying making her feel uncomfortable. He could sense her reaction—he had no doubt experienced it so many times that he made a game of it. But he had met his match in her. She wasn't interested—not one little bit.

'That's all right, then,' she smiled sweetly. 'What else would you like to know? My vital statistics, or have you got them sorted out too? You've certainly given me a thorough inspection.'

His lips quirked. 'Thirty-five, twenty-four, thirty-five. Height about five seven, weight approximately——'

'Okay,' she cut in, 'we needn't go into all the boring details. You've proved I hadn't underestimated you.'

'Dear lady, you would never be boring. On the contrary, you're quite a surprise. I didn't realise we had such a remarkable person working here.'

'But you did know of my existence, or you wouldn't have sent for me. When are you going to put me out of my misery? Have I got the sack or something?' It might be best if she had. Nathaniel Oakley was a lethal character; the longer she sat here the more clear it became.

Her bones felt as though they were melting and she knew that when she got out of the chair it would be an effort to walk. Her heart raced at twice its normal speed and perspiration caused her blouse to cling to her back where she leaned against the chair.

A heady scent of aftershave reached her nostrils, adding to the dizzying effect of simply looking at his superb body. He was some man, she had to admit.

He smiled. 'Even if I had considered dismissing you—which I haven't, I hasten to say—I would certainly change my mind. You're far too attractive to be tossed to one side. Have you ever considered becoming a model?'

So that was it! She ought to have guessed. He wanted her to pose for some of their advertisements. A pretty face and a good figure will sell anything—she had heard it all before.

But if he thought he was going to get her to blatantly use her sex appeal to advertise anything from a set of saucepans to a new car he had picked the wrong girl.

She shook her head so vehemently that her hair swung across her face. She pushed it back savagely, glaring at Nathaniel Oakley. 'No, I have not, and the idea doesn't appeal to me in the slightest.'

He leaned forward and stroked back a strand that had eluded her. She trembled as she felt his finger rest against her cheek for a few seconds longer than necessary.

She felt as though he was branding her, that when he removed his hand she would be left with a permanent mark where his finger had been.

Desperately she knocked him away. 'I don't think there's any need for that.'

'It was an excuse,' he admitted, with a show of humility she could not believe. 'An excuse to touch your hair. It fascinates me. I've never met a woman with hair that exact colour. It's like sunrise on a summer morning.'

What a way he had with words! Not surprising, though, considering the trade he was in. Words meant everything in advertising. The right words could sell almost anything to almost anybody.

But for him to speak to her like that was not in keeping with the big tough man she knew him to be. She had seen a glimpse of it when she first came into the room. She had heard talk of his hot temper and violent moods. He was being nice now, but for how long, and at what effort? He must want something very much.

'I'm glad you like it,' she said tightly. 'I don't, it's a nuisance. It refuses to be tamed.'

'A bit like its owner?' he suggested, grinning widely. He had very white teeth, made even whiter against his bronzed skin. Gisele wondered where he had got that incredible tan. Not in England, that was for sure, unless at a solarium, she thought nastily.

'Strange as it may seem to you,' she said, striving to keep her voice even, 'I do not usually lose my temper. Only on very rare occasions, when someone rubs me up the wrong way.' Like he was doing now.

'Then I must spar with you more often,' he said, reading her thoughts with uncanny accuracy. 'It suits you. Fire in your hair and fire in your eyes—a beautiful combination. Let's hope our relationship will be equally fiery.'

Gisele's heart stopped, everything stopped, and she looked at him, wide eyes fixed on the chiselled contours of his face. 'What do you mean, our—er—relationship?'

His slow smile did funny things to her heart. It began again, racing like a mad thing, beating against her ribcage so hard it hurt.

'I mean, Miss Latham, that you are my new secretary. Odette is leaving to get married. I'm quite sure we shall get on admirably. I think you're beginning to understand me, and I know I understand you.'

He pushed himself up and moved with panther-like grace to the front of the desk. Gisele watched as if in a daze as he lowered his head and very carefully kissed her on the lips. 'To seal the deal,' he whispered, and there was more than a hint of sensuality in his voice, a promise in his eyes.

Gisele blinked several times, told herself she was imagining all this, then shot out of her chair and out of his office. His wicked chuckle followed.

'Nine in the morning, Miss Latham, and be prompt. I cannot tolerate bad timekeeping.'

CHAPTER TWO

How Gisele made it back to her office she did not know. She was aware of Odette's startled eyes as she fled, the door banging as she swung it behind her, the sound echoing in her ears as she raced along the corridors and down stairs.

She could hear it still as she slumped in her chair, then realised it was her heart. It was hammering as though fit to burst. And not because of the exertion! Nathaniel Oakley had done this to her—the arrogant Nathaniel big-headed Oakley.

What type of man was he, to ride roughshod over her? How dared he presume she would automatically accept the position he offered? It had been a command. It had not occurred to him that she might not want the job. Did he treat all his staff like this, or had he singled her out for special treatment?

Her chest was still heaving and her eyes blazing when Bill Spalding came through into her office. He was a big bluff man with a red face and thinning hair. 'Well—did you get it?'

She eyed him suspiciously. 'You knew what he wanted yet you didn't warn me? Why? It was like being thrown to the lions—he devoured me! I had no choice. He told me I was going to be his secretary, full stop. I'm supposed to start in the morning.'

'Supposed to? Does that mean you don't want the job?' Bill sounded as though he found this difficult to believe.

Gisele shook her head.

'But I thought you had ambition? You keep telling

me how you're going to climb to the top. You're a good secretary, I shall be sorry to lose you, but this is too good a chance to miss. Nathaniel Oakley is very choosey. It's a great honour.'

'So am I choosey,' she declared strongly. 'And I'd rather work for you. Mr Oakley and I—well, I don't think we'd get on well together. He—he rubs me up the wrong way. He's too autocratic, too domineering. It wouldn't work, I know it wouldn't.'

'So what are you going to do? You can't just not turn up in the morning. He'd be down here like a shot.'

'And drag me along by my hair?' suggested Gisele, smiling wryly. She meant it as a joke but somehow felt he might do just that. She had a quick mental picture of Nathaniel Oakley's big brown hand knotted in her hair, herself being pulled protestingly along, no one taking the slightest bit of notice. They all realised that Nathaniel was Number One around here and whatever he wanted he got.

She was also aware of the warmth she had felt from his hand, the vibrations that ran through her at his touch, and she shuddered without realising it.

Bill Spalding looked at her curiously, grey bushy brows beetling above pale blue eyes. 'You're serious, aren't you? You really have taken an instant dislike to Nat Oakley. You shouldn't. His bark's worse than his bite. He's actually quite decent when you get to know him.'

'You're a man,' she said tightly. 'You think differently.'

He shrugged his big shoulders. 'I work for him the same as you. The same as everyone here.'

Gisele eyed him sadly. 'He eats women.'

Bill Spalding looked as though he was not sure whether he ought to laugh or not. He gave a tentative smile. 'He's good-looking, I suppose. It's natural he should have plenty of girl-friends. But from what I've seen so far he keeps business and pleasure strictly apart. You'll be quite safe.'

So why had he kissed her? Why had he touched her hair? It proved how little Bill knew the true Nathaniel Oakley. Maybe he hadn't so far dated any of the girls who worked here, but there was always a first time—and he had indicated that he felt more than a passing interest in herself.

Or had it been imagination? Had she, because of her heightened distrust of the male sex, read into the situation more than there actually was? Had it been nothing more than a gesture to make her feel at ease?

Her boss saw the uncertainty in her eyes and patted her shoulder awkwardly. He looked like a benign uncle trying to comfort his niece. 'It'll be all right, I know it will.'

'Such confidence!' she mocked.

He smiled ruefully. 'You deserve to get on, Gisele. You're a hard, conscientious worker. There are not many like you these days.'

'So what are you going to do if I go? Who's going to take my place? Mandy?'

Mandy was a standing joke. As a copy typist she was excellent, but give her anything that taxed her brain and she was out of her depth.

Bill shrugged. 'That's my problem. But if you're leaving me today how about getting this lot cleared up?'

Gisele was glad he kept her busy, it stopped her mind wandering. She concentrated fiercely, determined to push Nathaniel Oakley out of her thoughts.

But once work was over for the day and she was back in her flat, cooking her evening meal, she could dismiss him no longer. It amazed her how clearly she could remember him. It was as though his face had been indelibly printed on her mind.

She could recall with no effort those dark compelling eyes, the straight autocratic nose, thin yet sensual lips. There was no smile in her mental picture to relieve the harshness of his features, to soften the arrogant lift of his jaw. He was a tough, confident character, ruthless in his dealings with people.

It was unlikely he had ever suffered as she had suffered, as her mother had suffered. He was the type who caused the suffering, breaking hearts and pride as though they were of no more consequence than a matchstick. Once a match was lit it was of no further use. Once a woman was used—and abused—she was of no further consequence either.

Gisele stirred furiously, then realised that the sauce was thick and lumpy and not the least bit appetising— and she blamed Nathaniel Oakley for it.

She was a good cook normally, she enjoyed cooking, she enjoyed creating new recipes. What right had he to affect her in this way? She slung the contents into the bin and decided that fish on its own was unappetising and she would go out for a meal instead.

It was rarely she was so extravagant. She budgeted carefully, always putting a little on one side for a rainy day. But tonight she needed a boost. If she was to face that monster in the morning it was no good sitting here brooding.

To think that she had turned down a date! David Frazer, the financial wizard of the company, a new man brought in by Nathaniel Oakley, had tickets for a Beethoven concert and had asked her to accompany him. He was a thin serious man with thick hornrimmed glasses and not really her type. But he could be what she needed right now!

Impulsively she thumbed through the pages of the

telephone directory. She was probably too late, he would have made other arrangements, but there was always a chance.

Her fingers strummed on the table as she waited for him to answer. She began to think he had already left when the receiver was lifted and she heard his voice.

'David, it's me—Gisele,' she began eagerly.

He interrupted before she could say anything else. 'You've changed your mind?' He sounded delighted. 'You're coming after all?'

'If it's not too late?'

'Too late? I wasn't looking forward to going on my own.'

'I thought you'd have invited someone else?'

'There's no one I want to ask. I'll pick you up in half an hour and we'll eat first. How does that sound?'

'Marvellous!' she smiled, aware that she was being unusually enthusiastic, hoping he would not read too much into it.

David Frazer was a nice steady man. That was the trouble, he was too nice. He would never hurt a woman. He would love and cherish her, he would treat her like a Dresden china doll. He was not like her stepfather, or Adrian—or Nathaniel Oakley!

By the same token, his gentlemanly attitude made him dull. He would never set a woman on fire. She could enjoy a secure steady relationship, but that would be all.

Nothing like Nathaniel Oakley! Gisele shook her head impatiently. Why did her thoughts keep coming back to him?

She realised she was still holding the telephone, looking at it as if she expected Nathaniel to materialise from the mouthpiece. Quickly she slammed it down, as she had banged his door earlier. If he affected her like this before she began working for him, what chance did she stand once she was figuratively caught in his snare?

A cool invigorating shower helped, then she made up her face carefully, emphasising the natural beauty of her eyes with bronze shadow, darkening her sandy lashes, adding blusher to her cheekbones and colourless gloss to her lips.

She brushed her hair and fastened it into a coil on top of her head. It was the only way she could keep it in place, but even then annoying tendrils escaped, curling about her cheeks and neck.

Gisele did not realise that it softened the lines of her face, that it made her look feminine and appealing and a different woman from the one who wore her hair in a flaming mane.

Glancing at her watch, she saw she had only two minutes to finish dressing. There was a new dress at the back of her wardrobe, an impulse purchase. Unusual for Gisele, but it suited her so perfectly that she had succumbed, then stored it away for a special occasion.

Whether this was special enough was debatable. David Frazer was—well, not quite in that class. But he would feel flattered, and she would feel good, and that was what this evening was all about.

When the doorbell rang she was giving herself one last final rueful glance in the mirror. Was the dress perhaps a little too exotic for the occasion? Ought she to have worn something more discreet?

She sighed and opened the door. The expression on David's face was unbelievable. He was, she felt, like a cartoon character; she expected his glasses to shatter from shock. He looked as though he was staring at a vision.

'I'm sorry,' she said immediately. 'I guess this dress is a bit much. I'll go and change. Come in, I won't be long.'

David shook his head, stepping into the room as if in a dream. 'You're stunning! I always knew you were a good-looker, but tonight—you're sensational. Have you really dressed like that—just for me?'

Gisele caught her lip in her teeth and smiled shyly. 'It's for no one else. Do you truly like it? I thought perhaps——'

'It's perfect.' His eyes slid from her face down the length of her body. The soft material, like floating gold-dust, hinted at the feminine form beneath, highly provocative, yet revealing nothing. It had been outrageously expensive, but the designer had known exactly what he was doing. A pair of strappy gold sandals completed the outfit.

There was no insolence in David's appraisal, his eyes did not mentally undress her—as Nathaniel Oakley's had! Admiration, yes, and an owlish self-consciousness, as if he could not believe his good luck, but nothing else. 'Thank you, Gisele,' he said simply. 'Thank you.'

The restaurant was small and exclusive and David over-attentive. It was her own fault if she had given him the wrong impression, she decided ruefully, or rather Nathaniel Oakley's for forcing her into this situation.

If it hadn't been for him she would have been at home enjoying a piece of sole dressed up in a white wine sauce. Now here she was with David Frazer eating sirloin steak she did not really want, and wondering what on earth had made her do it.

She suddenly realised he was talking about Nathaniel Oakley. 'I've never known anyone quite like him. He's dynamite! He's building up a fantastic reputation for Thorne & Forest. Firms who have been using other agencies for years are changing over to us. In another twelve months we'll be one of the top agencies in the country.'

His enthusiasm left her cold. 'Have you known him long?' she asked.

'Years,' he said airily. 'I worked with him before. He's one of the nicest men I know.'

Nice? What a pitiful description! David was nice. Nathaniel was—objectionable. Also ruthless, arrogant and domineering. How could you possibly interpret that as *nice*?

Her eyes flashed. 'I met him today for the first time. I can't say I was impressed.'

David looked surprised. 'Then you're a minority of one. Women usually fall for his smooth charm. But in a way I'm glad he's not your type. If he was, there'd be no chance for me.'

He looked pleased with himself, so earnest, that Gisele knew she must put him straight. 'David,' she said softly, anxiously, 'don't build up your hopes. I could never—I mean, I was badly hurt by a man once, and I've no intention of becoming involved again. I'm a career girl now.'

He hid his disappointment bravely, though some of the brightness left his eyes. They were brown and sad as they looked at her through the lenses of his hornrims.

Involuntarily she reached across and touched his hand. 'It doesn't mean that I'm not enjoying myself. This is a super meal and I'm really looking forward to the concert.' Which was true, because she enjoyed music and Beethoven was one of her favourite composers.

'Will you come out with me again—no strings attached?' The hand which he placed on hers was cool and held none of the vibrant power she had experienced at the hands of Nathaniel Oakley.

It was as she had thought, David would never set a woman's pulses racing or her head spinning. Unless it was simply that she was not the right woman? She smiled gently. 'It would be unfair of me to promise anything, David.'

It was said that somewhere the right partner waited. She had yet to find hers, but she did know it was not David Frazer—nor indeed was it Nathaniel Oakley. Her reaction to him was a physical one. Her pulses raced with a passion of hate, a loathing for the type of man he was.

They finished their coffee and then it was time to make their way to the concert hall. They had good seats, and soon Gisele was lost in the world of Beethoven; David, Nathaniel, everyone forgotten. The first part drew to a close with the Emperor Concerts.

'That was wonderful!' She turned to David exuberantly, clinging to his arm as they joined the rush to the bar. 'I'm so glad you brought me.' She pressed a kiss to his cheek, laughing at his embarrassment.

He found her a corner and then went to get their drinks. There were so many people he had to shoulder his way through, and Gisele guessed it would be a while before he returned.

As she waited she became aware of someone watching her. It was more a sensation than anything else. Slowly she turned her head. She could not think how she had missed him; he was inches above everyone else.

His dark gaze slid over her contemptuously, then he murmured something to his companion and began to make his way towards her. The crowd opened up automatically, as though here was someone special. He did not have to force his way through as had David.

But if Nathaniel Oakley wanted to speak to her Gisele did not want to speak to him. Already a tingling feeling was speeding through her limbs, a faint warmth bathing her body.

Deliberately she made a pretence of looking for David, hoping Nathaniel might take the hint and go back. But she should have known better.

'A touching scene just now,' he sneered. 'How long have you been going out with Frazer? I must say he didn't seem too keen, you kissing him in public. Or haven't you yet found out that he's not the demonstrative type?'

Her head shot round—probably as he had intended. 'It was a thank you for bringing me here, that's all. David and I are just—friends.'

He looked amused. 'I didn't ask for an explanation. I'm not interested in what sort of a relationship you have. Except that, perhaps, I wouldn't have thought he was your type. He takes life far too seriously. I bet he's never had a taste of your glorious temper?'

Gisele eyed him belligerently, reluctant to admit that he looked pretty devastating in his evening suit. It emphasised his breadth of shoulder, made him seem even taller, the white silk shirt complementing his tan. He had a Latin look about him, and she knew he had a temperament to match.

'That's nonsense,' she declared hotly, thinking of Adrian and the way she had fallen for him. If anyone had been her type it was he—or so she had thought. How easy it was to misjudge!

'Oh, I don't know,' he said lazily. 'I reckon you and I would be pretty well matched.'

Gisele gasped. 'How do you make that out? You don't even know me!'

He smiled mysteriously. 'I know enough. I make it my duty to find out about each member of my staff.'

'You mean you spy?' It sounded typical of the man she was beginning to know.

He shrugged. 'I wouldn't put it that way myself. It leads to a better understanding. If Joe Bloggs is falling down on his job, but I know his wife's in hospital, then I don't take him to task. It's as simple as that.'

'And what do you know about me?' she asked tightly. Her pulse-rate had speeded up alarmingly, and her heart fluttered in her breastbone as though it was trying to escape. Why didn't David hurry up?

'Disappointingly, not a lot. You're a very reticent person, Miss Latham, or maybe you inspire loyalty? No one I contacted was prepared to talk about you.'

Somehow she did not feel he was telling her the truth. It was common knowledge she had been jilted and that plenty of men had unsuccessfully asked her out since. It was hard to believe they would not have mentioned it had he asked.

'So——' she said loftily, 'you're taking me on at face value? If I have a skeleton in my cupboard you know nothing about it?'

He grinned. 'It will be my pleasure, dear lady, to find out. And may I say how charming you look this evening? You've certainly done Frazer proud. Are you sure he's worth it?'

'He appreciates it, that's what counts,' she said primly.

'I'm sure he does. What man wouldn't? I'd be lying if I said I wouldn't like to be in his shoes. Perhaps some other time, Miss Latham?' The dark eyes rested on her questioningly.

Gisele tossed him a cold look. 'I don't think so, Mr Oakley. As I understand it, you never mix business with pleasure. Or was Bill Spalding wrong when he said that?'

His lips quirked. 'An unspoken rule of mine, I admit. But what are rules for, if not to be broken? You're a lady of exceptional qualities. I wouldn't have chosen you as my secretary if you weren't.'

Gisele was impulsive as well as hot-tempered, and she spoke without thinking. 'I may as well tell you, Mr Oakley, I have no intention of becoming your secretary. I appreciate you asking me, in fact I suppose I feel flattered, but it really wouldn't work. I couldn't possibly work for someone I *despise*.'

He drew in a quick angry breath, and at the same time his eyes grew flint-like, two lines creasing the space between them. 'My God, lady, you deserve dismissal for that! I will not tolerate insolence, do you understand? Perhaps you wouldn't mind telling me on what you base your opinion?'

The filmy material of her dress moved as she lifted her shoulders, moulding the contours of her breasts— a fact that did not go unnoticed by Nathaniel Oakley. 'You're a type I don't like,' she continued. 'Your reputation with women is—diabolical. Need I say more?'

'I think that's quite enough to be going on with.' The total anger in his voice sent shivers down her spine.

She looked about her desperately. Where *was* David? Surely it shouldn't take him this long to get a couple of drinks? She needed him; she needed rescuing.

Looking back at her companion she shuddered at the impact of those dark unnerving eyes, but was determined not to let him see that he intimidated her. 'I speak my mind. I'm sorry if you don't like it.'

For what must have been at least half a minute their eyes locked and held. Gisele was aware of all sorts of sensations dancing through her body, feelings she had thought were dead. They were fighting a mental battle, and strangely, she was enjoying it.

The scent of him was overpowering, a distinctive male smell that was personal to Nathaniel. And the long lean lines of his body sent out vibrations which came across in little shock waves—she felt each point of contact as clearly as if he were touching her.

She moistened her suddenly dry lips with the tip of her tongue—and remembered his kiss, and the touch of his finger against her cheek!

They had been deliberate attempts to arouse her, a way of leaving his own private calling card. He wanted her—not merely as his secretary—that was nothing more than a ruse. He wanted to take her to bed. For some reason that she could not imagine he desired her!

It was intriguing that this important powerful man should be interested in her, one of the lesser mortals in his well-run organisation, and she suddenly realised she was leaning slowly towards him. It was as if he drew her by some invisible cord, a strange magnetism that she could not feel but obeyed.

And he was smiling! He was watching her and smiling, no doubt anticipating the moment when their two bodies met. It took an effort to jolt herself back to normality. And when she did she stepped backwards, only to find someone pushing past, forcing her against the rock-hardness of the man she was doing her best to avoid.

His arms shot instinctively about her waist, protecting her from other would-be jostlers. She felt his hard-boned hips and muscular thighs thrusting against hers; she felt the powerful beat of his heart. And it came to her that he was as affected by this unexpected coming together as she herself.

She lifted her head to look into his face, caught an expression she could not understand, and struggled to escape. To her amazement Nathaniel let her go. Then she knew why.

'Sorry I've been so long.' David, flustered and hot, pushed a drink into Gisele's hand.

Nathaniel smiled sardonically. 'Don't worry, I've been looking after Miss Latham. We've had quite an interesting conversation.' He looked at Gisele. 'Don't forget, nine sharp. I shall expect you.'

David frowned when he had gone. 'Did I see him with his arms around you?'

'I was pushed against him,' explained Gisele, 'that's all. There are so many people in here it's unbearable.' Except that during the few minutes she had been talking to Nathaniel they might as well have been alone. She had been aware of nothing and no one except him.

'And what did he mean about expecting you at nine? Nine when?'

Gisele grimaced. 'In the morning. His secretary's leaving, and I've been invited to take her place.'

'He just asked you?' David sounded angry.

'No, this morning.'

He shrugged and looked defeated. 'It's a good promotion. I'm pleased for you.' But he was not happy, and he must have seen that the way Nathaniel Oakley held her was no accident.

Nathaniel had made the most of an unexpected situation—naturally, and the effect he had on her was disconcerting. No man had penetrated her defensive façade since the Adrian affair. So why had he? Why was he different?

'I've told him I'm not accepting.' She took a much-needed mouthful of her vodka and tonic and almost choked. 'I really couldn't work for such a man.'

His kind brown eyes widened. 'I shouldn't imagine Nat took that very kindly? And I'm surprised at you. What's happened to the career girl you spoke so proudly of? Becoming his secretary is certainly a rung up the ladder to success. It could be a stepping-stone to the board of directors. I've known it happen.'

Gisele shrugged. 'If it was anyone else I'd jump at the chance. I just don't like him.'

He lifted his brows but said nothing, and the next second the bell rang, warning that the second part of the concert was about to begin. Gisele finished her drink, thankful for the interruption, praying they would not encounter Nathaniel on their way back.

Her prayers were answered, but she did see him—three rows in front and a little to one side. She could not think how she had missed him before.

There was a girl with him. Not anyone Gisele knew—a slim brunette in a flame-red dress and eyes for him alone.

For Gisele the evening was ruined. No matter how she tried she could not keep her attention on the music. Almost of their own accord her eyes wandered time and time again towards Nathaniel.

In profile he looked proud and autocratic, which he was! He had a high noble forehead, a straight nose, and well-shaped lips. He was devilishly handsome, and his companion too seemed to have difficulty in concentrating on the performance. Frequently she turned to him and Nathaniel smiled and whispered, and the girl rested her head on his shoulder.

Gisele felt an unaccountable pang, which was puzzling when she hated the man. She wouldn't even have accepted him gift-wrapped on a silver plate. But the thought of some other woman being pressed against that exciting body, being the recipient of his kisses, luxuriating in the touch of his hands, was abhorrent.

She knew what his touch could do, what even being near him could do. It had sent her senses reeling and she did not even like him. If she did the whole world would explode.

Was this how the unknown brunette felt? Was her

stomach being churned into tight knots of desire? Was she impatient for the concert to finish so that they could be alone?

Gisele did not realise she had been staring at them for a full two minutes until David said quietly, 'The concert, Gisele. Don't let your hatred ruin the evening. Try to forget he's there.'

Easier said than done! She smiled ruefully and whispered, 'I'm sorry,' then made a determined effort to keep her attention on the performance. It was a sin to let Nathaniel ruin Beethoven.

But ruin it he did. She could not remember one note that was played during the last half, and the moment it was finished she said, 'Let's get out, quick.'

Everyone had the same idea, though, and it was difficult to push their way through. They had to be content moving slowly with the crowd.

They reached the street just in time to see Nathaniel Oakley's silver and red Porsche streak away. David smiled ruefully. 'I'm sorry I don't have his forceful personality. The crowds don't melt for me. But at least you've avoided him.'

So she had, she thought dully, wondering why she felt choked at the thought of Nathaniel and his girl-friend probably spending the night together.

David took her home and she invited him in for a coffee, knowing she need fear nothing, but he shook his head. 'No, thanks. It's been a pleasant evening. I'd like to do it again some time.'

She nodded, but knew this was the first and last time they would go out together. Nathaniel turning up had spoilt it. David did not altogether believe her story that she hated him on sight. And she had more or less given herself away when she kept looking across.

It was unlikely he would understand, even if she tried to explain. She was not sure she understood herself. How could her body react like this when she had schooled it so rigidly over the last couple of years?

Could it be that she was joining the ranks and was as physically attracted to him as everyone else? It was a disquieting thought. She certainly hoped it was not true. To have another disastrous affair would be the limit. She would lose her faith in human nature altogether.

CHAPTER THREE

GISELE had been in bed for no more than two minutes when the telephone rang. At first she ignored it, then when it became clear it was not going to stop she reluctantly pushed back the duvet.

Her voice was irritable, and she grew even more angry when she discovered who was at the other end.

'Miss Latham,' came the deep unforgettable voice of Nathaniel Oakley, 'did I disturb something? I'm sorry.'

'Are you?' she enquired distantly. 'Is it your custom to ring people at this time of night?'

'Only when I have something important to say.'

The fact that he sounded amused made Gisele crosser still. 'I can't imagine what's so important that it cannot wait until morning. On the other hand, you could have told me at the concert. Why didn't you?'

To her disgust her heartbeats quickened. How could a man affect her like this by simply talking on the phone?

'For the simple reason that something has cropped up since then. I shall be late in tomorrow. But Odette will show you the files, the general routine, etcetera, by which time I should be there myself.'

'And you phoned just to tell me that?' asked Gisele incredulously.

There was a pause at the other end and she thought she heard a woman's voice. So that was it, the brunette was his reason. She was spending the night with him and he did not want to rush away in the morning.

'I also want to give you a final reminder. It didn't

amuse me when you said you had no intention of working for me, nor did your reason. I found it most insulting.'

His voice grew hard and she could imagine the scowl that darkened his brow, the thinning of those mobile lips, but she also knew that it would not be long before he was in the arms of his lover and she, Gisele, would be forgotten.

'I expect you did,' she returned, surprising herself by sounding cool and calm. 'No man likes to be told that he's—unattractive to a woman. In fact I doubt many would have the temerity to tell you, even if they felt it. Like I said before, I happen to believe in speaking my mind. Good night, Mr Oakley,' and she put down the phone.

She half expected it to ring again, and in fact stood waiting for a couple of minutes. When it remained silent she shrugged and went back to her bedroom.

It was difficult to sleep after that. She had constant visions of Nathaniel and his girl-friend, and no matter how she tried to concentrate on other things, her mind always returned to that fascinating rugged face.

No other man had made such an impact on her. Even Adrian, with whom she had fallen wildly in love, had never haunted her thoughts to such an extent.

Nathaniel Oakley even intruded into her dreams. He became her cruel stepfather and her young prospective husband—different bodies, but always the same face. Coal-black enigmatic eyes, an autocratic nose with slightly flared nostrils, that well-shaped infinitely kissable mouth. And always in the end he let her down.

She woke feeling vaguely uneasy and thought at first it was the dream that disturbed her, then realised it was because today she began working for this notorious man. There had never been any doubt in her mind that she would ultimately agree to becoming his secretary, but she was glad her token gesture of defiance had let him see how she felt.

Unable to make up her mind what to wear, Gisele eventually decided on a grey skirt and white blouse, very severe and very plain. She buttoned a green bow-tie at the neck and slid her feet into high-heeled green shoes. She wore no make-up and held her hair back on her nape with a tortoiseshell slide.

The effect was totally opposite to the alluring young woman in the shimmering gold dress, and she wondered what Nathaniel Oakley would think.

Living no more than ten minutes' walk away from the agency, Gisele normally enjoyed her early morning stroll, sometimes going the long way round through the park, but today her legs felt leaden and the happy smile that usually lifted her lips was missing.

She arrived outside the building at five minutes to nine and took the lift up, meeting no one, which was unusual but suited her very well. Somehow she did not feel like talking about her new job.

The door to Nathaniel's suite was still locked, so she leaned back against it and waited. But when ten minutes had elapsed and there was no sign of Odette she decided to hang around no longer.

In fact it was a relief, or an excuse, and she felt much happier making her way down to Bill Spalding's office. A respite, no matter how temporary, was very welcome.

Bill looked at her in surprise as she sat down at her desk as usual, his kind round face puzzled. 'What are you doing here?' He sounded vaguely uneasy.

Gisele smiled wickedly. 'I can't get in. Mr Oakley's going to be late and Odette's not arrived. So I've come to help you.'

'If he turns up and you're not there he won't be pleased.' His concern was greater than her own.

She shrugged. 'That's his bad luck. If Odette's unreliable it's not my fault.'

Bill sighed and looked at her sadly. 'You're asking for trouble, Gisele. There must be a spare key somewhere, why don't you make enquiries? At least then he can't accuse you of not using your initiative. You do want him to be impressed? You don't want him to think he's picked a halfwit who's at a loss in an emergency?'

'I don't call being unable to get in an emergency,' laughed Gisele. 'Are you afraid for yourself, Bill?'

He gave a sort of half shrug. 'I did recommend you.'

Gisele smiled and stood up. 'Okay, if it will make you happy,' and she walked out of his office. But she had no intention of searching for a duplicate key. So far as she was concerned it was Nathaniel Oakley's bad luck if Odette chose not to turn up on the morning her replacement started.

Instead she decided to go and see David. On her way she met Ruth, and there was no ignoring the gleam in the other girl's eyes.

'What's this I hear about promotion?' she asked slyly. 'You're a dark horse and no mistake! Have you changed you mind about our new sexy boss?'

'Not in the least,' said Gisele haughtily. 'He's an arrogant, conceited pig and I hate him. To tell you the truth, I don't want his rotten job.'

'Then why did you take it?'

Gisele shrugged. 'I had no choice. It was an order. It was either that or get fired.' Even though he had not exactly said this she felt sure it would have happened. Nathaniel Oakley did not like being crossed.

'We're all green with envy,' said Ruth, pushing open the door to the typing pool. 'Come on, tell us what happened. Why did he ask *you*? Why not me?' She patted her hair and took an admiring glance at herself in a mirror perched on top of the filing cabinet. 'I wouldn't say no.'

Helen, Sally and Mandy all looked at Gisele with something approaching reverence. 'Come on, tell us what he's like!' 'What did he say?' 'Is he as sexy close up as he is from a distance?' The questions came thick and fast.

Gisele could not help laughing. 'Hold on, I didn't ask for any of this! Bill put my name forward, but I wish he hadn't. I can't stand the thought of working for Nathaniel Oakley. He makes my skin crawl!'

Ruth shook her head. 'I can't believe you feel like that. You really have got a hang-up about men, haven't you?'

Gisele nodded. 'I can't trust any man again. Not his sort. I don't mind working for Bill, he's comfortable. He'd never make a pass. But I wouldn't trust Nathaniel Oakley any further than I could throw him.'

'It does give you a wonderful opportunity, though,' said Ruth thoughtfully. 'I've often heard you say how you'd like to get your own back on men like Adrian. Now's your chance.'

Gisele frowned. 'I don't understand. You're suggesting I—use—Nathaniel Oakley—for revenge. How?'

'It's easy,' smiled Ruth. 'Get him to fall for you, and then drop him—like Adrian did you. You said yourself that he's the type to discard women when he's finished with them—so why not do it to him? I bet it's never been done.'

'And I'm not going to be the one to do it,' protested Gisele. 'You're insane even suggesting it!'

'Are you scared?' asked Helen.

'Or afraid you might actually fall in love with him?' Sally added.

There was no fear of that. 'I just don't happen to want to lose my job,' returned Gisele primly. 'I might not like working for the guy, but it's a step up the ladder, and that's all I'm interested in.'

She was clearly not believed. 'You *are* scared,' crowed Ruth. 'Goodness me, it's a golden opportunity. Go on, do it—I dare you. Think what it will do for your morale!'

An awful lot, if the truth were known. It was a tantalising thought—but no, it wasn't worth losing her job simply to get one over on Nathaniel Oakley.

'We dare you as well,' said Helen and Sally.

Mandy merely nodded, but her eyes glowed, and Gisele knew she was in full agreement.

'You're mad, the lot of you!' she snapped. 'I have no intention of getting involved with Nathaniel Oakley, or any other man—*ever*!'

Ruth looked disbelieving. 'There's a tenner on it. Does that tempt you?'

'Off each one of us,' added Helen.

'Now you're talking,' said Gisele, deciding it was easier to go along with them. Not that she had any intention of doing anything so ridiculous, but she had to shut them up somehow.

She left them chattering excitedly as she carried on to David's office. He sat at his desk behind a huge pile of papers, his round owl-like eyes widening even further when he saw Gisele.

'Good morning, David,' she said brightly. 'I've come to thank you again for taking me to the concert. It was a lovely evening. I really enjoyed it.'

He looked at her warily, not deceived for one minute by her cheerful attitude. 'Why are you here? You're not——' He stopped, as though it was too awful to contemplate. 'Gisele, he'll give you your cards! You can't do this to a man like him.'

She smiled sweetly. 'David, calm down, you've got it wrong. I did go, but I couldn't get into the office, so I've come to see you instead.'

'You could have waited,' he said plaintively.

'Why should I? If and when he eventually turns up he can come and find me. Oh, you didn't know, did you? He phoned last night to say he'd be late. Something important in the form of a brunette cropped up.'

'He said that?' David looked surprised.

Gisele shrugged. 'Not exactly, but that was the gist of it. It's typical of the type of man he is. He has a one-track mind. Sex! Sex before breakfast, sex for breakfast, and sex after breakfast, and not necessarily with the same woman.'

'Gisele, stop it!' David pushed himself up and came round to her, putting his hands on her shoulders and looking worried. 'You're getting yourself worked up for nothing.'

'I am not worked up!' she declared belligerently. But she was. Her stomach churned. She had never wanted to be Nathaniel Oakley's secretary, had been forced to resign herself to the fact that there was no way out unless she wanted to lose her job, and being messed about like this did her no good at all.

'You're very uptight,' he said. 'Shall I get you a coffee? Will that help?'

She shook her head. 'It's nerves, that's all. I didn't know I had any until I met Number One.'

He frowned. 'Number One?'

Gisele grinned. 'My nickname for Nathaniel Oakley. It's his initials, don't you see? It's all over his car, so why not call him it? Number one super-stud, I shouldn't wonder.'

'Gisele!' David was shocked. 'That's not——'

'It's all right.' Nathaniel's clipped tones jerked them apart. David looked as though he wished himself anywhere but there, but Gisele, though inwardly quaking, looked at the big dark man boldly.

'Miss Latham has already told me in no uncertain terms what she thinks of me, Frazer. She's merely confirming it.' His face was as cold as ice, eyes unblinking, jaw inflexible. 'I think you'd better come with me.'

Before she could object he gripped her arm and led her forcibly from the room. She glanced helplessly at David over her shoulder, but instead of the sympathy she expected, his expression was one of resignation. She had brought this on herself, it said, now she must accept the consequences.

Outside David's office she struggled furiously, her earlier fanciful thoughts about him dragging her along by her hair flooding to the surface. 'Let me go!' she snapped. 'What are people going to think?'

His eyes flashed darkly. 'If they're of the same mind as you, probably that I'm going to rape you. You disgust me, Miss Latham, do you know that?'

She disgusted herself. It had been silly and childish and she couldn't think why she had said it. But no way was she going to let this despicable man know that.

Abruptly he released her, and she drew a deep breath of relief. Her arm tingled where his lean powerful fingers bit into it, and she was more vitally aware than ever of his devastating masculinity. It did not seem fair that one man should possess so much power.

His long easy stride took him along at such a pace that Gisele had almost to trot to keep up with him. 'Why were you wasting time in David's office?' he rasped. 'Didn't you have enough of him last night?'

It occurred to her that he thought David was the reason she had been so long answering the telephone. David's hands on her shoulders just now must have confirmed it. Why disillusion him? 'It seemed the obvious place to go when Odette didn't turn up,' she explained.

'Odette's here now,' he snapped, and she saw the angry gleam in his eyes.

'She was late,' said Gisele pointedly. 'Doesn't she know that you're a stickler for time-keeping, or is it only me that you're inflicting your rigid rules upon?'

He glanced at her coldly, but did not stop his rapid pace. 'Everyone, but everyone in this company is expected to be here on time. Unless there are extenuating circumstances. Why should you be any different? Odette unfortunately got caught in a traffic jam following an accident. There was nothing she could do about it.'

Gisele decided the time had come to hold her tongue. She might not like Nathaniel Oakley, but she had got to work with him.

The rest of the morning went quickly. She was kept so busy that she had no time to think about Nathaniel Oakley. Apart from taking him a cup of coffee at eleven she did not even see him.

After lunch, which she spent as usual eating her sandwiches first and then going for a brisk walk to revitalise her system, he called her in and proceeded to dictate a whole batch of letters at a speed that left her no time at all to think of Nathaniel, the man.

He was a high-powered business executive—precise, detached, and extremely competent. It was clear he expected competence in his secretary as well. Gisele's pencil flew across the pages until her fingers ached and her neck ached and she wondered when it was going to end.

At length Nathaniel sat back, linking his hands behind his head, looking at her with a superior smile on his handsome face. 'That should keep you going for a while. Did you manage to get it all down?'

'But of course,' she replied coolly. 'You wouldn't have chosen me if you hadn't known I was up to it.'

A dark brow slid up. 'The proof of the pudding is in the eating, so they say. I'd like them to catch the five o'clock post.'

Gisele gasped. 'You're joking! I shall do most of them, certainly, but not all.'

'Bill said you were quick.' He looked at her steadily and she was unable to tear her eyes away. 'Prove it!'

'You can't get blood from a stone,' she snapped. 'I shall do my best, I can't do more.' The atmosphere was claustrophobic. It was a big room, but even so she felt choked. Now that her mind and fingers were no longer occupied she was very much aware of Nathaniel. The sheer masculinity of him sent her senses reeling. It filled the room with waves from which there was no escape. It was a heady sensation and one she had never experienced before.

It frightened her so much that she shot to her feet like a startled rabbit and backed towards the door, her eyes still on his face. A smile lifted the corners of his lips and she felt he knew the reason behind her sudden movement.

'I'll make a start, she said huskily, groping behind for the door handle, then shooting through into the outer office the second she opened it.

His deep chuckle followed her, a sensuous sound that set her nerves tingling anew. But she determinedly put aside all thoughts of what he could do to her and concentrated fiercely on the job he had set her to do.

A client came to see Nathaniel and Odette disappeared somewhere, so Gisele was left completely alone. Her fingers had never flown so quickly over the keys of a typewriter. She amazed herself, but was more than satisfied to see each accurate, neatly set-out letter. He should have no complaints.

At half past four she had finished. It was a feat she had not expected to accomplish, and she gave herself a mental pat on the back. At five Nathaniel was still tied up with his client—and the letters unsigned! She had dared to poke her head round his door, but he banished her with a glance.

At half past five it was time to go home. She looked at the letters angrily. It was infuriating, to say the least, after all the effort she had put in.

The next day was no better, and by the end of the week Gisele felt exhausted. He really was dynamic, not letting up for one second, and expecting his secretary to maintain the same crippling pace. Work was uppermost in his mind at all times. He saw her as a cog in a wheel, not a human being.

So much for that first impression! All he had been doing was conditioning her. He knew she would be flattered if he paid her some attention, and now that he had caught her in his snare, so to speak, he no longer cared.

Odette left and the pressure increased, but Gisele was by now getting used to Nathaniel Oakley's method of working and often anticipated his needs, actually beginning to enjoy herself.

Bill had been right when he said Nathaniel never mixed business with pleasure—and this suited Gisele. It would be impossible to work with him if sexual feelings were involved—on either side. As things stood it was perfect. She was another step higher up her career ladder—and Nathaniel was completely satisfied.

It was a bombshell, therefore, when he visited her home a couple of weeks later. Gisele was so shocked she simply stood and stared. Whoever she had expected when her doorbell rang it was not him.

He filled the doorway, an impeccable silver-grey suit moulding itself to his powerful body, accentuating each and every muscle. He was different from the automaton who ran Thorne & Forest with such superb efficiency, he was once more the sensual male who had held her against him on the night of the concert, and again dizzying waves threatened to consume her.

His eyes probed her curves beneath the kaftan she had slipped on for comfort, and she flushed and stepped back into the room. 'I don't know what you want, but I suppose you'd better come in.'

'I've had better invitations!' His lips twisted wryly but he came in all the same, looking about him with genuine interest. He unbuttoned his jacket. 'May I?' and without waiting for an answer he shrugged out of it and hooked it on a stand near the door.

'You're making yourself very much at home,' Gisele said tightly. 'How do you know I'm not expecting visitors?'

'Dressed like that?' Amusement flickered in his eyes. 'Unless it's Frazer, of course. Do you entertain him often?'

She lifted her chin. 'I don't see that my private life is any concern of yours.'

He sat down, filling the armchair. 'Mmm, I like it here, it's comfortable. Nicely decorated, nice furniture. Have you chosen it yourself?'

'Some of it, some belongs to the flat.' She stood near the door, still wondering why he had come.

'Sit down.' He waved his hand expansively. 'There's something I want to discuss with you.'

Gisele moved warily across the room, turning off the television and taking a chair as far away from him as possible.

'Wouldn't it wait until tomorrow?' she asked huskily, surprised to hear herself sounding breathless.

'I prefer to discuss it tonight.' His steady dark eyes were fixed on hers, an undecipherable expression in their depths. She sensed that whatever had brought him here was important.

'How would you feel, leaving all this?' Again he looked at the comfortably furnished room with its deep armchairs and rust-coloured carpet which almost matched her hair.

She lifted her chin characteristically and gave him a sharp glance. Now what was he up to? What devious thoughts were going through his mind? 'I wouldn't,' she snapped. 'I've worked hard to get this place how I want it, and I don't intend giving it up—for anyone.'

He did not look perturbed. 'I rather thought you'd say that. Perhaps you'd better listen before you start jumping down my throat.'

'I doubt whether any propositon of yours would interest me,' she returned coolly. Why was he spoiling what had promised to be a perfect working relationship?

'It might,' he said. 'You're a woman first and foremost, with a woman's heart and a woman's feelings. You pretend to be cold, but I suspect that deep down you're warm and compassionate.'

He paused to judge the effect of his words. Gisele stared at him, frowning slightly, her smooth brow creased, her green eyes puzzled. 'Compassionate? Or do you mean passionate? You're not inviting me to live with you, by any chance? Has your dark-haired beauty let you down?'

'Don't flatter yourself!' he thrust angrily.

Gisele felt her cheeks flush with shame. Too late she wished she had thought before she spoke. It should have been clear that this was not what he had in mind. Nathaniel might enjoy a mild flirtation, but that would be all. No serious commitment.

She stood up. 'I've got some coffee on. Would you like a cup?' It was imperative she get out of the room. She had made a fool of herself and she needed a few minutes to regain her composure.

He inclined his head, smiling now, aware of the thoughts racing through her head. It entertained him to see her in a dither. It made him feel even more superior than he normally did. How she would like to hit him!

She scuttled into the kitchen and closed the door, leaning back against it and drawing several deep breaths. Her limbs shook with a combination of anger and humiliation. How could she have said such a thing? How could she?

Not until she felt steadier did Gisele load a tray with cups and saucers. When she returned Nathaniel had put on a record. He looked very much at home and there was no hint on his face that she had spoken out of turn. It helped, although her hand when she poured the coffee was not quite steady.

She pushed his cup across the low table. 'Help yourself to cream and sugar.'

He did, looking with distaste at her own black, sugar-free drink. 'No wonder you're so skinny!'

'Is that what you think?' she enquired tartly, then realised that she had left herself wide open again.

He smiled. 'Not really. I suspect you have curves in all the right places, except that you always seem to wear clothes that conceal them. Is that deliberate?'

Gisele thought of the flame-red dress his companion had worn the other night. It had revealed more than it concealed, but was certainly not her choice. She had a good figure, she knew, but why flaunt it and give men the wrong impression?

'No one's complained,' she said. 'Besides, I please no one but myself.'

'Not even Frazer?' Nathaniel suggested softly.

He would never know the concert had been a one-off occasion. 'Not even him,' she said levelly, sipping her coffee, wishing he wouldn't look as though he was mentally undressing her.

'What a peculiar woman you are!' He leaned back in his chair, still studying her, causing her pulses to race unaccountably. 'Were you very upset when your fiancé jilted you?'

The unexpectedness of his question made her spill coffee into her saucer. So he had been lying when he said he knew nothing about her. 'What's that to do with you? You ask some mighty personal questions.'

'I'm interested in people.'

She eyed him hostilely. 'As a matter of fact, yes, I was,' she said defensively. 'I was brokenhearted, just as any bride would be if she was let down on her wedding day. What did you think, that I'd a heart of stone and could shrug it off as one of those things?'

'Do you still love him?' His voice was low-toned and serious.

Gisele shook her head. 'It was a long time ago.' She could have added that because of Adrian, because of men like him, she had no intention of ever falling in love again.

But when her heart was suddenly working overtime, when every nerve-end was vitally aware of this magnificent male specimen dominating her room, how could she declare such a thing?

She had not felt like this since her affair with Adrian finished. It was as though her frozen heart was starting to melt. But why now? And why because of this man, of all people?

'And David, how do you feel about him?'

Why was he asking all these questions? They could be of no real importance. Where were they leading? 'I've not yet had time to form an opinion,' she said tightly.

Nathaniel smiled enigmatically, his dark eyes calling her a liar. 'How long does it normally take you to get to know a man? Does your body respond to him as it does to me?'

'I don't—it doesn't.' Panic rose inside her. She swallowed convulsively and stared at him, her beautiful green eyes wide, her body suddenly rigid. 'You're very conceited if you think that!'

'Put down your cup and I'll prove it.' He eased himself out of his chair and moved towards her. Gisele watched as if mesmerised, noting the thrust of muscle against the smooth material of his trousers, the absolute confidence.

He was powerful, too powerful if he chose to force himself upon her. With hands that trembled she clutched her cup and saucer defensively. 'Mr Oakley, no! What are you doing?'

'Trying to prove a theory.' His voice was soft and dangerous. 'And let's forget the Mister, shall we? We're not at work now. It's Nathaniel, or Nat, if you like. That's what my friends call me.'

'I'm no friend of yours!' she retorted, frantically trying to stem her rising hysteria.

He stood over her, taking the cup and saucer from her nerveless fingers and placing them on the table beside his own. 'You could be.'

'I don't want to be.' She shrank back into her seat and stared up at him with wide startled eyes. Her heart was racing fit to burst. 'Why don't you tell me why you came and let's get it over with?'

'All in good time—Gisele.'

Crazily she liked the way he said her name. He made it sound different, special.

He held out his hands and she looked at them but dared not touch. They were long, lean and tanned. His fingers were square at the ends, nails short and immaculate. They were strong and capable, and she had seen them many times before and thought nothing. Now she could not help wondering what it would feel like to have them caress her.

The very thought made her chest tighten, her breathing difficult. Her mouth was dry, her lips too. She ran the tip of her tongue over them and looked up to see Nathaniel's eyes had darkened.

'Gisele!' He put a hand on either side of her chair, and there was no escape. 'You're one hell of a sexy lady beneath that cool façade. Why don't you relax? You can't keep men at bay for ever just because of one unfortunate experience.'

She closed her eyes, trying to blot out this madman who was daring to tell her what she wanted. But the exciting male smell of him could not be ignored, nor the touch of his leg against hers, his warm breath on her cheeks.

Her lids snapped open and she discovered his eyes mere inches from her own. They were not so black as usual; they were smoky grey, outlined with a thin black line round the iris. The whites were very white and his lashes thick and sooty. His distinctive aftershave teased her nostrils and there was a confident smile on his lips, as if he was very sure he was going to get his own way.

Instinctively Gisele pushed her hands against his chest, aware of the tight wall of muscle beneath her palms, but more intent on escaping than admiring his physique.

His smile widened and he caught her hands. The next second she was on her feet and he had slid an arm behind her back, pulling her resisting body embarrassingly close. Once again she felt his long, lean male length, but this time there were no crowds to protect her.

She saw his head begin to descend and tried to twist away, but he was quicker. His mouth found hers in a kiss that was surprisingly gentle, though all the more devastating because of it.

Gisele had half expected this to happen ever since she saw him standing in the doorway, but she was not prepared for the sensations it created.

The wall of defence she had so carefully built, which had proved sufficient when fending off other male predators, was nowhere near strong enough to keep this man out. It slowly cracked, allowing him to penetrate, causing fingers of excitement to spread through her nerve-streams, filling her with trembling anticipation.

And it was wrong. This man, above all others, was a type not to be trusted. It was his sort who caused the heartache, the unhappiness, the despair.

She meant nothing to him. He was merely playing a game, a dangerous game—and she wanted no part of it. He must never know he had the power to break down her barriers. With a strangled cry she twisted away.

CHAPTER FOUR

GISELE faced Nathaniel, looking at him with a half-scared expression. Her legs felt boneless, her heart thudded so loud she felt sure he must hear. 'Why did you do that?' she whispered.

He gave a warm intoxicating smile that seemed to encompass her and pull her yet again into the circle of his arms. She could almost feel the pressure of his body against hers, and her breasts tingled where they had been crushed against his hard chest.

She closed her eyes in an endeavour to shut him out. In that one brief moment he had made her more aware of her own sexuality than even Adrian had. It was ludicrous! She had thought herself beyond that sort of thing. For years now she had schooled her body not to respond to any man—especially men like Nathaniel Oakley.

He was the type who used a woman, who took advantage of her weakness, who raised her to the heights—and then unscrupulously discarded her.

'Has no one ever told you that you're irresistible?' His voice was deep and sexy and he looked in no way put out by her rejection. 'Isn't it obvious why I did it?'

He took a step forward and Gisele backed hastily, feeling a chair behind her and sitting before her legs crumpled. He knew! He knew exactly what he had done to her.

'It's not obvious at all.' She tried to make her tone cross, but it was difficult when her heart fluttered, when simply looking at him sent all sorts of unwanted sensations pulsing through each and every nerve. 'I suspect you make a pass at every woman you meet.'

'Only when they're as beautiful as you.' He stood over her and she realised it had been foolish to sit down. She was at his mercy again.

'And I imagine you shoot them all the same line?' she returned heatedly.

Nathaniel pretended to look hurt. 'You think I'm not serious? You think I don't consider you beautiful at all? Gisele, shame on you! You're exquisite. You're any man's dream. If no one's told you that before they're idiots. And the guy who decided not to marry you must be either blind or the biggest fool of all.'

'I'm sure he'd be flattered,' said Gisele tightly. 'Why don't you sit down and let's discuss whatever it is you came for?' He was suffocating her with his nearness, making her tingle with the vibrations emanating from his virile male body. He was far too dangerous for her peace of mind. She had been quite happy in her world without men. Why was he trying to ruin it? Her job too—didn't he realise how difficult it would be working for him after this?

'If that's what the lady wants.' He moved reluctantly, his eyes never once leaving her face.

Gisele felt like screaming. He was stretching her to breaking point and enjoying every minute. She had never before come up against a man with quite so much confidence in his own ability to arouse a woman.

He sat down, lowering himself slowly, almost as though each movement was designed to draw attention to his long muscular limbs, as though he was showing her what she was missing, suggesting that his body could be hers if she so wished.

Gisele closed her eyes and unconsciously shook her head, rejecting him, trying to dispute the erotic image he projected. Her hands clutched the arms of her chair, drawing some comfort from the solid inanimate object beneath her fingertips.

After a few deep breaths she looked at him. He was watching her from beneath hooded lids; patient, content to wait all night if necessary for her to regain control of herself.

He must feel very good, she thought irritably. Her reaction must have given a tremendous boost to his morale. But it would not happen again; in future she would keep a strict rein on her emotions. She would rebuild her wall and no one, no one, would break it down.

'Are you ready to talk?'

His softly spoken words added fire to the smouldering anger that had begun to take over. 'I've been ready all night,' she snapped. 'You're the one who's messing around!'

His well-shaped brows rose. 'You could have worded that better, but I won't argue. The crux of the matter is, I want you to come to Cornwall with me.'

Gisele's mouth fell open. 'Whatever for?' What devious thoughts were going through his mind now?

'To work, obviously. You really are a good shorthand-typist. Bill wasn't kidding when he said you were the best. Will you come?'

'No!' she said flatly.

'Why not? You don't even know what's involved.'

She sighed. 'I'm not interested. I don't want to go to Cornwall, or anywhere else. I'm pursuing my career here very nicely, thank you.'

'Perhaps you might change your mind if I tell you what's involved?'

'I doubt it.' But it did intrigue her. Was it an affair he wanted after all?

He frowned, looking momentarily angry. 'You're so damned stubborn!'

'I don't like being pushed around,' she said coldly. 'It's my life, I'll do with it what I want.' Why was he so persistent?

He raised a jet-black brow in amusement. 'You didn't get married when you wanted.'

Gisele drew in a hissing breath. 'There are some things over which a person has no control. I made one mistake, I shan't make another.'

A calculating gleam came into his eyes. 'Meaning it might be a mistake getting to know me?'

'Precisely,' she snapped. 'I've already made it clear how I feel about you. You and your type are abhorrent to me. I have no intention of going to Cornwall with you and getting involved in—in a relationship I don't want.'

His lips quirked. 'Is that what you think? Actually, I want you to work for my sister, not me.'

Her head jerked. 'Then what excuse is there for you to go?'

'None at all, except that I could do with a break. Pulling Thorne & Forest out of the mire was no mean feat. I've worked hard and long hours—I reckon it's time I took a couple of weeks off.'

Gisele looked at him warily. Her body had more or less returned to normal; no longer did she feel on fire. 'What does your sister do?' It was a reluctant question born of curiosity, not because she had any intention of working for the woman.

'You may well ask. Not very much at all.'

Gisele frowned. 'Then why does she need me?' He was talking in riddles.

'Because it will help her.'

'Because for some devious reason you want to get me down there? That's it, isn't it?' she demanded crossly. 'You're making up a job so that you can drag me away from here. What's wrong, haven't I fallen at your feet like everyone else? Is your ego hurt? Do you think you might get somewhere with me if the surroundings are more romantic?'

'Shut up, damn you!' Nathaniel said sharply. His brows drew into a straight black line above eyes that were suddenly and surprisingly sad. There was a tautness about his mouth that had not been there before, and his thoughts had clearly drifted a long way away.

It was several minutes before he spoke. When he did he was barely in control of an emotion that ravaged his body. 'I was in a very bad car accident a couple of years ago. My mother died, my sister was crippled, and I—I got away scot-free.' He spoke through clenched teeth, despising himself, full of an agony that revealed itself with the pain in his eyes.

Gisele stared. 'Nathaniel, how awful! But you can't blame yourself. You——'

'I was driving,' he interrupted harshly. 'Don't you see, it was my fault? I sometimes think the guilt of it will drive me out of my mind.'

She shook her head. 'It could have happened to anyone. Just thank the Lord that you're alive.' Her wide eyes were full of horror and sadness and a strange desire to comfort him. For once she was the stronger of the two.

'That's what Catherine says.' He got impatiently to his feet and turned his back. 'She's a remarkable person. She ought to hate me, instead she loves me more than ever. She ought to be bitter because she's confined to a wheelchair, instead she's more cheerful and good-tempered than any person I know.'

He whipped round and glared at her. 'I want to help make something of her life, Gisele. I owe it to her. That's why I need you.'

Her eyes almost filled her face as she looked at him.

There were not many people, she guessed, who caught a glimpse of this side of Nathaniel. It made her feel humble. 'I appreciate you asking me,' she husked, 'but I'm a secretary, Nathaniel, not a nurse.'

'Damn it, she doesn't need another nurse!' he grated. 'What she does need is someone to get down on paper all the incredible ideas that spin around inside her head. She dreams up stories so powerful it's a crime not to record them.'

'She can't write either?'

He shook his head bitterly.

'And you're suggesting I take them down in shorthand and transcribe them later?'

'That's right. We've tried a tape recorder, but she freezes. There's no spontaneity when using a machine. If you could be there on hand for when these ideas occur, it could make all the difference to her life. She would feel better, it would give her something to live for; not that she's ever given up—she hasn't, she's quite phenomenal.'

'But why me?' insisted Gisele, slowly pushing herself up.

'For one thing,' he said, 'because I know you're capable. You can work under pressure and you can work at high speed. Catherine tends to go on and on when she gets started. You'd certainly need stamina. But mainly it's because I think she'd like you—it's that simple. Since her accident she fights shy of meeting strangers, but I'm sure she could communicate easily with you. Do you think you could do that? Would it upset you seeing her in a wheelchair? Would you feel awkward? If so, there's no point, but——'

Gisele shook her head. 'It wouldn't bother me. I feel so sorry for her, I——'

'She doesn't want pity,' he thrashed savagely.

'Catherine's a finer person than you or I will ever be. She occasionally get cross, but for the most part she's an angel. She makes me feel very small. You probably grumble when you have a headache. Catherine is in constant pain, but she never says anything.'

'She sounds a very exceptional lady,' said Gisele quietly, almost reverently. 'How old is she?'

'Twenty-five. She'd have been married by now. It was all fixed. When it was discovered she would never walk again her fiancé didn't want to know.' The way he clenched his fists made Gisele wonder whether he hadn't punched the man in question into unconsciousness.

Gisele had thought herself hard done by, but her experience had been nothing compared with this brave woman's lot in life. A lump rose in her throat, threatening to choke her, and tears stung the back of her eyes. 'Nathaniel, what can I say?'

He caught her shoulders roughly. 'Say you'll do this job for me.' His deep eyes searched her face, but for once there was no sensualism in them. A sense of urgency, a desperate wish for her to agree, but sex was the last thing on his mind.

Gisele felt she was being trapped. He was playing on her sympathy. And the truth of the matter was she did feel sorry for Catherine, desperately so. She could imagine no worse fate than losing the use of your limbs while your brain still functioned normally. It was like being a prisoner within oneself.

And to have her fiancé reject her because of it must have been the cruellest blow of all. Didn't it confirm her own thoughts exactly? What a selfish lot men were!

'How long would it be for?'' she asked softly. 'I don't want to give up my career. It's important to me.'

Nathaniel lifted his broad shoulders. 'Who's to say?

For as long as Catherine needs you. I mean, she might not even want you there, in which case you'd come straight back. As I said, she's not happy about meeting people. She doesn't mind relatives, but she hates the thought of complete strangers seeing her incapacitated. Why is your career so important? I thought that to most women it was a stopgap until they got married.'

Gisele tossed her head. 'I have no intention of getting married. I'm aiming at something—managerial.' She eyed him defiantly. 'If I leave Thorne & Forest there's no saying I'll find another job easily—not on the same level.'

'So you'd put your own needs before those of my sister?' He looked angry all of a sudden.

'Why shouldn't I?' frowned Gisele. 'I don't know Catherine, neither do you know whether she'd accept me. It's a gamble all round, and not one I'm prepared to take.'

Nathaniel gave an impatient sigh. 'Look, Gisele, I give you my word that there'll be a job for you at Thorne & Forest when Catherine no longer needs you. You won't be demoted, I promise you that. Now, will you come?'

It was tempting. She would feel mean if she didn't do it. And it would certainly be a change. So long as she did not lose out by it. She was looking forward to carving out a career for herself in advertising.

'Catherine needs the stimulation,' he said, sensing she was weakening, pressing home his advantage, 'otherwise she'll grow into a cabbage.'

'Does she know you plan to foist me on her?' asked Gisele. 'Was it her idea that you look for someone to write down her ideas?'

'Heavens, no!' he said quickly. 'If you agree I shall introduce you as a—er—friend of mine, the rest must come as a result of natural progression. She hates to think she's putting anyone to trouble. She's the most selfless person you're ever likely to meet. I must warn you, it could take time before she's prepared to confide in you. You'd have to give up this flat, of course,' he added. 'There'd be no point in hanging on to it.'

Gisele looked at him sharply. 'That's it, I can't go! I couldn't do that. I can't afford to let it go. I'll never get another one like it. Have you any idea how difficult it is to find a decent place—within my price bracket, anyway?'

Nathaniel shook his head angrily. 'Gisele, you're just making excuses. I'll pay you well, you won't have to worry about money.'

But Gisele was adamant. She was not giving up her independence. She had no intention of relying on him if she could find nowhere to live when the job came to an end.

'If you feel like that,' he said at length, 'then sub-let it. I'll ask my lawyer to draw up a contract—that way there'll be no problem when you do return. Some people have a nasty habit of refusing to leave.'

He was removing the obstacles one by one; she had no argument left. 'I suppose,' she said, 'it wouldn't hurt for, let's say, six months. But no more.'

'Unless we find that Catherine really can't do without you?' There was pleading in his eyes that she had never expected to see.

'I can't promise,' she said faintly.

Nathaniel let out a deep relieved sigh and pulled her against him, and she buried her head in his chest. She felt his hands stroke her hair, and it was satisfying to know that she had pleased him. All the antagonism had gone, and they were sharing a sadness, perhaps even building up an understanding.

She had no idea how long they stood there. It

seemed like eternity. Then he gently put her from him. 'I think we both need that coffee now. Sit down, I'll put the pot on to heat up.'

It never occurred to her to resent him taking charge. It seemed natural that he should. Nathaniel was built that way. Gisele turned over the record that had long since finished and curled up on the sofa.

She thought about Catherine, wondering whether she had the same compelling looks as her brother. If she did, she would be a handsome woman, and it was all the more lamentable that she was committed to life in a wheelchair.

It was easy to understand Nathaniel feeling as he did. She would probably feel that way herself. He would never be able to rid himself of his guilt complex, not so long as he lived. And seeing Catherine must surely drive it home even more forcibly.

He returned with the coffee, his face back to normal, with no hint of the self-inflicted torture, no suggestion that anything tragic had ever marred his life.

'Here we are,' he said cheerfully. 'Shall I play mother?'

He sat next to her, his bronzed hands, with their film of tiny dark hairs, big and capable, making her coffee black as she liked it, heaping sugar and just a little cream into his own.

Gisele leaned back in her corner, the pale green couch a perfect foil for her red hair and black kaftan. Several strands of her hair were caught and held by the pile of the fabric. Nathaniel leaned towards her and teased them away, treating each as though it was as fragile as a thread of silk.

They drank their coffee and talked some more, then Gisele yawned. Immediately Nathaniel jumped up and said perhaps it was time he went. 'We'll go down at the weekend, that will give you a couple of days to sort yourself out.'

She walked with him to the door. He turned and took her into his arms, holding her very gently. 'Thank you, Gisele. I'm sure you won't regret it.' Then he went, and she was left with a vague feeling of disappointment.

The next two days were hectic. Nathaniel kept her busy clearing up neglected paperwork, organising, making sure everything would be covered while he was away. She did not have a spare second to see Ruth, David, Bill, or anyone.

At home she spent her time frantically packing, borrowing a couple of cases, cramming shoes into supermarket carriers, toilet things into spare handbags. Going away for six months was like moving house!

On Saturday morning Nathaniel arrived early, freshly shaven, a crisp white shirt hugging his chest, pale blue denims moulding his thighs. It was the first time she had seen him in anything other than a suit, and she was shocked anew by his raw masculinity.

He looked at her luggage with an amused lift to one dark brow. 'A typical woman, I see—everything but the kitchen sink!'

Gisele returned his good-natured bantering. 'I'm coming prepared.'

He grinned and tucked two cases beneath his arms, picking up another in each hand and striding towards the door without the least indication that they were heavy.

Gisele scooped up a couple of smaller bags and led the way down the flight of stairs. Expecting to see the gleaming silver Porsche, she was surprised to find a blue estate car instead. It was new and luxurious and registered, NO 2.

For a second she stared, then lifted her head to

discover him laughing. 'No, I don't have three and four as well.'

Gisele tried to look serious. 'I never for one moment thought you had. Whatever gave you that impression?' But she could not stop a smile in her eyes.

She had grown to like Nathaniel over these last few days. His concern for his sister told her he was not the uncaring sort of man she had at first thought.

He had made no further physical demands on her either, and this was the way she wanted it. She could enjoy being Nathaniel's friend—but not his lover. There was no doubt in her mind that his lovers were cast off like last year's fashions.

Once her luggage was loaded she took one last look around and locked up, leaving the key with her neighbour as arranged. She had the strangest feeling that one part of her life was over and another just beginning, that nothing would ever be quite the same again.

She soon discovered that sitting in the close confines of the car was very different from working together in the office. Suddenly there was no escaping Nathaniel's magnetic sex appeal.

His long legs were stretched out in front of him, denim taut across hard muscles. The steering wheel slid expertly through lean brown fingers. The sleeves of his shirt were rolled back to reveal tough sinewy arms.

When he changed gear his hand came dangerously close to her thigh, so close she was sure she could feel the warmth from it, and she certainly felt a tingle of shock.

It had never occurred to her it would be like this. He had been so impersonal at work that she had forgotten how easily he could arouse her.

Without realising it she edged towards the door. He

gave her a dark look, but the next time he changed gear and she visibly flinched he jerked coldly, 'What the hell's wrong?'

She shot him an oblique glance, noting the harsh lines grooved in his face, the straight mouth, the tense jaw. 'I—er—nothing's wrong. Why should there be?'

His eyes flicked over her angrily. 'Because I've got eyes in my head. What is it, Gisele? What have I suddenly done to make you like this?'

Desperately she shook her head, her fingers nervously pleating her cotton skirt. She could hardly tell him that it was herself she was afraid of, that it was the feelings he was able to arouse inside her without even trying.

'I suppose I'm a little nervous about meeting Catherine,' she improvised. 'I mean, she might not like me—then all this will be for nothing.'

'And the thought of that's making you shrink away from me as though I'm a leper?' Nathaniel laughed harshly, grimly. 'I'm not a fool, Gisele, don't take me for one. Do you think I'm abducting you or something? That I've spun you a tale that hasn't a thread of truth in it, and am about to carry you off to some remote part of Cornwall to have my way with you?'

'No, of course not,' she denied quickly, afraid to look at him, glancing instead at the buildings flashing quickly past. It was a bright sunny day in midsummer. She should be singing for joy. Why then was her heart filled with lead?

'But you are afraid of me?' he insisted, honking his horn furiously as a car pulled out in front.

She caught her lower lip between her teeth, wondering how she was going to get out of this without making a fool of herself. 'Not you personally——' she began.

He groaned. 'God, don't say we're back to that old thing again! I'm not your type—okay, I know it. Perhaps you wouldn't mind telling me what your type is, then we might just begin to understand one another?'

Gisele was silent and he glanced at her impatiently. 'Is it David? Is he your type? I hope not. I've known him for a long time and he's excellent at his job, but so far as anything else goes he's out of the running. Or is that what you like, a meek and mild man without an ounce of sex appeal? Is it sex you're afraid of? Once bitten, twice shy, you don't want to get involved again, is that it?'

When she still refused to answer, he continued savagely, 'Don't worry, I have no designs on you. I like my women with a little more warmth. I thought that with your red hair you'd have a passion to match, but I found out the other night that you haven't—so you're quite safe. You don't trust men, that's the top and bottom of it. You had one unfortunate experience and you're letting it ruin your whole life.'

'Can you blame me?' she asked huskily. 'I've never been given any reason to think otherwise. Men use women for their own selfish needs. They revolt me!'

'I see.' He clenched the wheel a little more tightly, knuckles gleaming white through his skin. 'Thanks for telling me. It will make me doubly careful in future to keep my hands off you.'

Gisele closed her eyes, feeling cold inside. To be truthful with herself, she did not want Nathaniel to ignore her. She wanted to feel his hands exploring her body, she wanted to feel his total maleness against her. It was insanity when she had tried so hard to condition herself into hating men, but she was attracted to him whether she liked it or not. A tremor ran through her.

When the brakes squealed and she was shot forward

in her seat she opened her eyes quickly. 'If that's how you react to me, Gisele, I think we'd better call this whole thing off right now.' His lips were curled back thinly from his teeth, skin drawn tight across fleshless cheekbones. She had never seen him look so inflamed.

It took a second or two to work out that he was referring to her involuntary shudder. 'That wasn't because I despise you,' she said quickly. 'I was thinking about something, that's all.'

'Something that made you look as if you were terrified out of your wits?' he asked coldly. 'Perhaps you wouldn't mind telling me what it is?'

She shook her head. 'I'm sorry, I can't. It's kind of private.'

'Concerning me?' he blazed, eyes like black coals searing into her.

She bit nervously on her lower lip. 'Sort of, I suppose, but not in the way you're thinking.'

'How the hell do you know what I'm thinking?' he growled. 'You're making a fine mess of all this, you know that? We can hardly turn up at Catherine's sworn enemies. Either you have a quick change of attitude right now, or I'll turn round and that will be an end to it.'

She thought of his sister, of the wonderful character he said she was, her bravery in the face of her illness. She thought how confident he had been that she was the perfect person to help Catherine make something of her life. Why should she, Gisele, allow her own small insignificant feelings take precedence over what this woman must have suffered? It was a case of priorities—and conscience! If she let Nathaniel's sister down she would never forgive herself.

She looked at him and managed a weak smile. 'I'll try.'

'You're sure?' he crisped, eyes narrowed.

Gisele nodded.

'No more hysterics if I come near you?'

'No,' she said quietly.

'Good. I rang Catherine this morning and told her we'd be arriving today. There is just one thing—as I said, she fights shy of anyone outside our immediate family seeing her, so I told her you were my fiancée, and to cover up the fact that I'd not mentioned you before I told her that I'd swept you off your feet—that it was love at first sight.'

CHAPTER FIVE

'You did what?' Gisele's beautiful green eyes filled with horror.

'I think you heard very well.' Nathaniel looked at her calmly, unemotionally. There was a rigid hardness to his jaw, his lips thin and grim.

She had heard, oh yes, but he had no right doing this without consulting her first. It was despicable. 'You have a nerve!' she snapped angrily. 'Why go that far? I can't possibly pretend to love you, not feeling the way I do.'

A slow smile curved his lips but did not reach his eyes. They were dark and angry, and Gisele guessed he had not thought she would react so violently. 'Then I shall have to work on you,' he said quietly. 'Somehow, between now and arriving at Stormhaven, I have to persuade you to change your mind.'

'Never!' There was an electric tension in the car, so great that Gisele would not have been surprised had sparks shot between them. 'You shouldn't have said that without telling me!'

'I never realised you'd be so damned difficult. I thought you felt compassion for Catherine. I thought you wanted to help?'

'I do,' she insisted, curling her fingers into her palms in an endeavour to stop their trembling. 'But not at this expense!'

His grey eyes glittered as he leaned towards her. 'It's necessary, to convince Catherine you're there for no other reason than as a future member of the family. Do you really despise me that much?' He was so close his warm breath fanned her cheek—and there was nowhere to go! Already her back was pressed against the door.

Gisele tried to hold his gaze, but her eyes fell before his compelling power. When his hard-boned fingers imprisoned her chin, lifting her head until once again she looked at him, she could not contain the quiver that ran through her at his touch.

It was as though the electric current was now in full force, making her tingle but go rigid with shock at the same time. His eyes never left hers as with slow deliberation he leaned further towards her.

As his mouth got closer Gisele drew in a harsh shuddering breath, steeling herself for the impact, knowing it would be a mistake to let him kiss her, that he might yet again begin to crumble her carefully resurrected defences.

As he misinterpreted her reaction Nathaniel's eyes grew ever harder and darker, the frame of black lashes accentuating their hostility.

When his lips touched hers Gisele let out a cry of anger, ignoring a swift, unexpected, *unwanted* response, and balling her fists she pummelled his chest, one blow following another with the rapidity of a boxer in training.

A sneer curled his lips as with effortless ease he caught her wrists in his free hand, holding them against his chest where she could feel the hammer-blows of his heart. He was by no means as cool as he looked.

Her chin felt as though it was being bruised as his pincer-grip tightened. But when he kissed her all pain was forgotten. It was a brutal, ruthless kiss, intent only on punishing. Even so, it aroused in Gisele a gamut of emotions that rose from her stomach to her throat, threatening to choke her with their intensity.

His hand left her chin to hook itself behind her head, while his mouth moved with ever-increasing hunger across her lips. Fingers of flame licked through each and every limb, despite all her efforts to stop them.

She knew it was imperative to hide her involuntary reaction. Nathaniel was one of that breed of men who never had any difficulty in arousing a woman, especially when it suited their own ends. If he knew how she felt there would be no stopping him.

Catherine was the motive in this instance, nevertheless there was no need for him to do this. There had been no need for him to declare that they were engaged. Friends would have done, like he had said in the first place. The odd kiss she could put up with, but this—it was offensive and unnecessary, and in no way enamoured her to him.

With an iron will she kept herself stiff, determined not to respond, not to reveal by so much as the flicker of a pulse that he affected her.

His mouth scorched an impatient trail of kisses across her face, lingering against the delicate area behind her ears, burning a course down her slender neck to plunder the soft hollow of her throat.

Throughout it all Gisele sat impassive. It was hard to pretend she was unmoved. Her body was more vibrantly alive than she could ever remember, responding of its own accord to Nathaniel's advances, even though her mind ordered it otherwise.

Just when she thought she could last out no longer he thrust her from him savagely. 'Don't think I'm fooled by your ice-woman tactics,' he breathed hoarsely. 'You can't keep up your guard for ever. But I fear this is neither the time nor the place to work on you further.'

He jerked back into his seat, raking tense fingers

through his jet-black hair, flinging her one last bitter glance before starting the engine.

It was not until then that Gisele realised they were still in a busy main street, and that they had aroused the interest of more than one passer-by. One elderly woman in particular looked at them with so much disgust that Gisele's cheeks flamed with humiliation.

She sat back primly, rearranging her skirt, trying to appear unconcerned. Taking a peep in the vanity mirror on the sun-visor, she was appalled to see how wild and dishevelled she looked.

She searched her handbag for a comb and tugged it through her unruly hair, then gave up and folded her hands in her lap.

Nathaniel drove in silence. She had expected him to shoot through the streets at alarming speed, instead he impressed her by keeping well within the limits. His hands were relaxed on the wheel, and daring to glance at him, Gisele was amazed to see the hint of a smile curving his lips.

But on taking a second look she realised his smile was completely devoid of humour; merely bitter, derisive, as though he was planning his next move.

He gave no indication that he saw her looking at him, keeping his eyes on the road ahead, flicking occasionally to the rear-view mirror, then back again to the front.

Not until they were out of the suburbs and on the open road did he put his foot down. The car responded immediately, surging into throbbing, pulsating life—much as she had minutes earlier!

It was an incongruous comparison, but true all the same. Nathaniel handled the car with a delicate touch, gently persuading it into action. He would treat a woman in the same way, and ninety-nine per cent would probably react as the car did now, performing in exactly the manner he expected.

Gisele was the one per cent that was different. She had a mind of her own. Like an old banger she would need to be coaxed into action, treated with something more than the indifference most men used towards their possessions—whether they were girl-friends or cars did not seem to matter.

If Nathaniel wanted her to pose as his fiancée it would take more than a few rough kisses to persuade her. Much to her disgust she knew she was capable of being coaxed, but not unless he treated her with more consideration. She refused to be sexually bullied into a situation she had wanted no part of in the first place. In fact she could not imagine why she was letting Nathaniel Oakley use her in this manner, after all the heartache she had suffered, after all the vows she had made.

For at least an hour neither of them spoke, the powerful car effortlessly eating up the miles. But the silence was uncomfortable, and at length Gisele could stand it no longer.

'Tell me where we're going,' she said. 'What part of Cornwall?'

'The west coast,' he replied, 'not far from Padstow. Do you know the area?'

The deep tones of his voice filled the car, but the hardness had gone; it was again inflected with the sensuality that had thrilled her the first day she had heard him through his office door.

As on that occasion it sent tingles through her limbs, made her realise how easily she could succumb to the innate power of this man. She looked at him, letting her eyes feast themselves on the strong lines of his face. 'I don't know Cornwall.'

'You've never been? Cornwall—the most romantic of all counties? Gisele, your education is sadly lacking.' He glanced across, his smile rueful. 'It will be my pleasure to be your teacher.'

For a second, before he turned his attention back to the road, their eyes met. She saw mockery, but something else too, that caused her stomach muscles to painfully contract.

She was glad it was no more than a fleeting glance, because it had been a look designed to accelerate her pulses. Nathaniel was letting her know that he found her desirable even though she scorned his advances.

Part of his plan of campaign, no doubt, so that she would be capable of effectively pretending to be his fiancée. Ironically, it worked. She was vitally aware of the long exciting body close to hers.

'The part of Cornwall where Catherine lives, where I used to live, where I was born and bred, is untamed,' he told her. 'The cliffs are unchangeable, as dangerous as the sea itself, with a wild splendour that's second to none.

'Most of the county has been taken over by tourism, it's lost its raw beauty, but not on the headland at Stepper. You'll either hate it or love it, Gisele. It's a wild and lonely place, with no one but the seabirds for company.'

'I suppose it could be—interesting,' she said. 'Fine in summer, but not so much fun in winter. Do you get cut off? Doesn't your sister mind? I should have thought that in her condition she would prefer somewhere more civilised.'

Nathaniel flashed her a dark look. 'Wait till you meet Catherine. Then you'll realise that her spirit is as indomitable as the cliffs. She's at one with them. She relishes nothing more than to sit on the headland with the wind and rain blowing in her face. She knows every inch of the area. As a child she ran barefoot through the heather and climbed the cliffs fearlessly. Losing the use of her legs was the cruellest thing that could happen.'

There was a white line round his mouth as he again mentally chastised himself for what he had done, and Gisele guessed he would carry this burden for the rest of his life.

'She sounds quite a woman—I'm looking forward to meeting her. But why don't you tell me something about Padstow? You said it was your nearest town.'

It was with an effort that he diverted his thoughts. 'Padstow is an ancient town with a long and interesting history, but I won't bore you with details. It's built on an inlet, nestling under an old sea cliff, sheltered from the gales that blow on as many as thirty-five days a year.'

Gisele pulled a face, but let him continue.

'At Stormhaven we have no shelter, but the house is built to withstand the roughest of storms. It's centuries old and capable of standing for a few more. It's quite something to be in the house when a gale blows, when the Atlantic beats against the cliffs and the water boils and erupts with an anger more violent than anything you've ever seen.'

A bit like Nathaniel himself, thought Gisele. He had a quick temper that was like none she had witnessed. Except perhaps in James? But she tried not to think about him. If it hadn't been for his violent moods her mother would be alive now. And she wouldn't be here! It was strange how fate worked.

'Padstow itself, though,' continued Nathaniel, 'is sheltered in the lee of the cliffs and has a surprising climate. You'll be surprised at the number of exotic trees and shrubs that grow there. If you feel the loneliness of Stormhaven too much, Padstow is the place to go. All the older buildings huddle round the harbour. It's an interesting jumble of houses and restaurants, of artists' studios and gift shops, holiday flats and bookshops.'

Gisele smiled. 'It sounds delightful. I've seen postcards of quaint Cornish villages. I can't wait to explore.'

He nodded indulgently. 'It's a much slower pace than you're used to. Everything slows down in Padstow. It has to. The streets are too narrow for cars to go rushing around, and a lot of people's lives are governed by the tides, or the seasons. I sometimes wish I'd become a fisherman instead of joining the rat race.'

'What made you leave?' she asked.

He shrugged. 'Why does anyone? My parents weren't well off, but they struggled to give me a decent education. I went to university and after that there didn't seem much point in returning to Cornwall, so I decided I could help them better by making something of myself in London and sending them money instead.

'Naturally I went home as often as I could. We were at one time a very close-knit family, but then Father died and my younger brother went to Australia. That left my mother and Catherine. I'm afraid my visits home grew less frequent. I tried to persuade them to move to London, but prising them away from Stormhaven was like trying to part a limpet from a rock with your fingernails.

'They finally agreed to come for a holiday, the first time either of them had ever visited London.' His breathing grew ragged, and Gisele saw again the white of his knuckles.

'The accident?' she whispered, uneasily. 'It was then that it happened?'

He nodded. 'We hadn't even got there. Some damn fool braked for no apparent reason in front of me. The result was a nasty pile-up with us in the middle. Catherine had to be cut out of the car.' He shuddered, in the grip of an emotion he was powerless to do anything about.

Gisele guessed that speaking about the accident was the only time he ever lost his superb self-control. 'What can I say?' she husked. Impetuously she laid a hand on his arm. 'Nathaniel, please try to——'

With an impatient gesture he knocked her away. 'For heaven's sake don't humour me! It's over and done with, but it's one hell of a thing to live with. You'd never understand, not in a thousand years.'

She compressed her lips and looked sad, racking her brains for something else to talk about. But it all seemed to come back to this same thing, which was inevitable, considering she was going to try and help his sister.

But she did understand—more than he thought. She knew what it had felt like when her mother took her life. In a way she blamed herself for this, feeling that perhaps she could have helped, could have smoothed the way between them instead of resenting her stepfather and often trying to intervene, which had only succeeded in making matters worse.

Again there was silence as the car ate up the miles. Gisele wondered whether Nathaniel would stop for lunch, but as they passed through Somerset into Devon, and finally into Cornwall itself, it became apparent that he intended finishing the journey in one go.

He pointed out Jamaica Inn as they crossed Bodmin Moor. Gisele had read Daphne Du Maurier's novel of that same name and longed to ask him to stop so that she could see for herself the setting of that haunting melodrama; the scene of Mary Yellan's horror and torment, the home of big Joss Merlyn, her uncle and landlord of the inn that was a cover for strange goings on.

But he drove now with grim determination, and she wondered whether he had forgotten that he had threatened to make her respond to him before they reached their destination.

They eventually passed through a beautiful tunnel of trees into Wadebridge, over a lovely arched stone bridge, and on through the town. Gisele was fascinated by everything she saw. This was Cornwall, wild and dramatic Cornwall, her home for the next six months.

After another two miles they branched off the main road and headed for Padstow. The road was narrower here, hedged with green. They passed through a village with the delightful name of Little Petherick, with charming cottages and gardens full of roses, a church and a pub, people walking or talking.

Then they came to another main road that led to the town itself, but they turned off this and gradually the lane narrowed into nothing more than a dirt-track. By this time Gisele was on the edge of her seat, looking about her eagerly, marvelling at the freshness of it all. The green was so green! Everything was so vivid and clear, with none of the haze that muted the scenes of London.

She held her breath when she caught her first glimpse of the sea. Aquamarine, turquoise, azure—what colour could she use to describe it? It was a combination of these and more. It danced and sparkled where the sun kissed its surface, it disappeared from view and then allowed her to catch only tantalising glimpses through breaks in the trees and shrubs that clung fast to the undulating headland. The trees were bowed by the harsh winds of time, stunted, their backs broken by the force of nature.

It made her feel very small and very insignificant. It was wildly primitive, breathtakingly beautiful, and she could understand Catherine wanting to live here for ever.

There was no comparison between this and London. London stifled. Here was fresh air and freedom. It was like being in a different world.

When a huge grey stone building came into sight Gisele knew instinctively that it was Stormhaven. As they drew closer she could see that what had originally been quite a small house was extended to make it into a rambling, interesting home. Creepers grew over it, flowers surrounded it, and as Nathaniel stopped the car and they climbed out, she suspected that love blossomed inside it.

There was a feel about it that reached her even as she stood and looked. It was a place to be joyful in, a place that had known both happiness and heartache, but in which happiness had triumphed.

Catherine was right to stay here, she knew that now. To live anywhere else after she had experienced Stormhaven would be like spending the rest of one's life in prison.

She laughed out loud for the sheer joy of being alive and turned a happy smiling face to Nathaniel. 'It's beautiful—and I haven't seen inside yet. Oh, Nathaniel, I'm so glad you brought me!'

He immediately took her into his arms. 'Stormhaven does have that effect—on the right person.'

'And you knew I'd like it?' Gisele's pink lips were parted as she tilted her head and looked into his eyes.

He caught his breath and brushed them with a tender butterfly-light kiss. 'It's the red hair that told me. It's as untameable as these cliffs, as wild and exotic as Cornwall itself.' He caught it between his hands, lifting it from her head, letting it float like cloud on the breeze.

Gisele sensed the change in him. He seemed at

with the elements, as though he was a part of this
corner of England, as though its very strength ran
through him, as though he had been born of the land
itself.

He seemed stronger and taller and more overpowering, yet at the same time strangely gentle. He
took her arm and led her forward. 'Let's go and meet
Catherine—I saw her face at the window. She'll be
impatient. She'll wonder what's keeping us. Though
when she sees you, my lovely Gisele, she won't
wonder at all. Have I ever told you you're beautiful?'

She dimpled and felt suddenly warm and wanted,
and wondered whether she had done wrong to keep
her heart packed in ice all these years. Nathaniel here
was different from Nathaniel in London. It would be
easy to forget her antagonism, easy to forget she had
sworn never to fall in love again. There was an
indefinable something in the air that was already
weaving its magic. She would have to watch herself.
Nevertheless she put her hand into his and together
they walked towards the house.

A ramp led to the front door, designed, she guessed,
for Catherine's wheelchair. The hall was long and
high-ceilinged, with oak-panelled walls and a marble-
tiled floor. They walked along its entire length,
Gisele's heels making a sharp sound, Nathaniel's
rubber-soled shoes silent.

At the end they turned into a room that was filled
with sunshine so brilliant that for a moment Gisele
was blinded. It was not until Catherine spoke that she
realised Nathaniel's sister was sitting a little way back
from the window, but in such a position that it
afforded her a clear view of the rugged coastline and
the mighty ocean beyond.

She looked into a smiling face that was nothing like
had expected. There was no resemblance to

Nathaniel at all. Catherine had corn-gold hair, a delicate heart-shaped face and the bluest eyes Gisele had ever seen.

She appeared fragile, as though a puff of wind would blow her away, yet there was a strength of character also apparent which must have been the Oakley inheritance. But more than that, there was an aura of serenity about her, of contentment. She looked at peace with herself and with the world.

Nathaniel was right, she bore him no grudge. On the contrary, she loved him dearly; there was a light in her eyes as she looked at him that came from an inner happiness.

He bent low and folded her into his arms, and he was so big that she seemed to disappear altogether. He swallowed her up, this man who was her brother, who suffered agonies each time he saw her, each time he thought about her, but who loved her with every breath in his body.

Gisele felt a lump rise in her throat and tears filmed her eyes. This was a private reunion of which she had no part, but it made her realise that Nathaniel was as caring and vulnerable as everyone else when it came to the ones he loved. He had assumed a surface veneer of toughness, of ruthlessness, but it was no more than a shell to protect the man inside.

Lifting his head, he beckoned to Gisele. 'Come and meet my sister, the most wonderful person in the world. Catherine, this is Gisele.'

'The new love in your life?' Catherine glanced at Gisele self-consciously, her delightful husky voice tremulous. 'She must be quite someone to make you propose so soon! Hello, Gisele.' She held out her arm awkwardly, a silver ring with a lapis lazuli set in the centre of its intricate moulding seeming almost too heavy for her thin fingers.

Gisele moved forward and took the offered hand, impulsively pressing a kiss to the woman's cheek.

Catherine looked startled, then pleased. 'Welcome to Stormhaven, Gisele. We love this place, Nat and I. I hope you'll love it too.'

'I do already,' said Gisele. 'I sensed it the moment we arrived. It has the sort of atmosphere that reaches out and takes you into its arms.'

'That's Catherine, not the house,' said Nathaniel, smiling fondly at his sister.

'Take no notice of him,' laughed Catherine. 'He's an old flatterer. But I expect you already know that? I can't get over it—Nathaniel engaged! It's about time somebody put a stop to his gallop.' She had quickly got over her initial shyness. 'I'm dying to know how it happened!'

'Where's Meg?' Nathaniel put a stop to her questions. 'Gisele and I are starving. In my haste to be with you, my darling sister, I stopped for nothing and no one.'

'She's had lunch ready this past hour,' said Catherine in her gentle husky voice, which was as much a contrast to her brother's deep tones as was her appearance. 'Grumbling as usual. You know what she's like.'

He grinned. 'I'll fetch our cases, then go and find her. Gisele, I expect you'd like to freshen up?'

'I'd prefer to talk to your sister first,' she said hesitantly, 'if you don't mind?' She was fascinated by this remarkable woman who took pain and hardship in her stride.

Catherine nodded. 'I'd like that too. Give us a call, Nat, when you're ready to eat.' When he had gone she said, 'You're not at all what I expected. I always thought Nat had a penchant for voluptuous blondes.'

Gisele shrugged. 'Perhaps he felt like a change?'

'I think,' said Catherine slowly, 'that at last he's come to his senses. I saw straight away that you're right for him. It will be lovely having you here. I hope you're going to stay a while. This isn't a flying visit?'

'If you'll have me, I'd love to,' smiled Gisele, squatting on a tapestry stool and drawing her knees into the circle of her arms.

It was impossible to tell by Catherine's attitude that she could not walk, that those slender legs clad in sheer stockings and elegant slippers were incapable for evermore of carrying her weight. It would be a privilege to help her make something of her life.

'If I'll have you? Of course I will. It's my own fault I don't see anyone, but I can't bear pity. You know about the accident?'

Gisele nodded. 'I think you're very brave. I also think it's a cross Nathaniel's going to bear for a long time.'

Catherine tossed her head with just a shade of impatience. 'I don't know why. It could have happened to anyone. Actually, I'm surprised you know. You gave no sign of it on your face. Did Nat warn you?'

'He told me about you, naturally,' said Gisele carefully, 'but I don't see it as any reason to treat you differently from anyone else.'

'I think I'm going to like you,' said Catherine happily. 'I felt it straight away, isn't that funny? I've had my fill of so-called friends who, because I can't walk or do very much for myself, think I'm an imbecile as well. I'm much happier with just my own family around me—and you're going to be one of them. I'm so glad Nat met you.'

'He was very anxious to get here,' admitted Gisele, 'now I know why. He loves you very much—and you have such a lovely home. I can understand you never wanting to leave.'

'It is nice,' Catherine admitted. 'Have you been to Cornwall before?'

Gisele shook her head. 'But I love it already. It's so dramatic, so full of mystery. I wanted to stop at Jamaica Inn, but I was afraid to ask Nathaniel. Now I'm glad I didn't. I'm glad we came straight here. You're the angel Nathaniel said you were.'

'Not always,' admitted Catherine ruefully. 'Sometimes I fly off the handle like anyone else. But I do try to be as independent as I can. It's fun sometimes trying to do something that's seemingly impossible. And when I succeed I feel so proud. But let's not talk about me—tell me about yourself. How did you meet Nat?'

Gisele was not sure how much Nathaniel had told his sister. She hoped he hadn't made up some complicated story. 'I work for Thorne & Forest,' she explained.

'Oh, that new agency he's always talking about,' said Catherine quickly. 'What do you do there?'

'I'm his new secretary.'

Catherine pulled a face. 'I don't expect Nat will want you to work once you're married. Personally, I think a woman should be allowed to follow her career if that's what she wants. Hey, I've just noticed, you're not wearing a ring. Hasn't he bought you one yet?' She sounded incredulous.

Gisele shrugged. 'It was so sudden, and there was so much to do before he could get away. I don't think he even thought about it.'

'Shame on him!' said Catherine quickly. 'Why is it that men don't realise how much these things mean to a woman? You'll have to be firm with Nat, or he'll walk all over you.'

Gisele grinned. 'Don't worry, I can look after myself.'

'Meaning the sparks have already flown?' asked the

other girl discerningly. 'Good for you! I've seen his girl-friends in the past fall over backwards to be nice to him. They grovel—it's positively sickening! You'll never do that. Perhaps that's why you two clicked. Perhaps he realised that at last he's found a woman of character.'

'Perhaps,' agreed Gisele, wondering what Catherine would think if she knew the true story. It made her feel guilty to be so readily welcomed into this house.

It was a relief when Nathaniel returned. "Lunch will be on the table in five minutes,' he informed them. 'I'll show you your room, Gisele.'

'You were right,' she said, as they mounted the stairs. 'She's unlike anyone I've ever met.'

'And you got on well?' The question was anxious. 'She certainly didn't seem to mind me bringing you—which is a good sign.'

'We took an instant liking to each other,' admitted Gisele, 'so you needn't be afraid that your little plan is going to fail. If we carry on like we have these past ten minutes she'll be confiding her stories in no time at all.'

'Good, good,' he said positively, but without warmth. 'I'm glad I made the right choice.'

Gisele felt some of her buoyancy fade. He made it sound as if he had picked her from a long string of applicants for a job that was just a bit different, and he had not been quite sure whether she was the right person.

How could he expect her to act the part of a loving fiancée if he treated her with cool detachment the moment they were out of his sister's hearing? It was bad enough having to pretend to love him, without him making it worse.

But he was adept at that, as she had already learned. Whenever he wanted something, he used his sexuality. Any other time she might as well not exist. Exactly what had she let herself in for?

CHAPTER SIX

NATHANIEL left Gisele at the door to her room. 'When you're ready, straight downstairs, second door on the left.' He was gone before she had time to answer.

She sighed, lips compressed, and made her way inside. How difficult it was going to be!

But her low spirits did not last long. It was a delightful room, a summer room, full of white and blue, green and gold. They represented blue skies, ripening corn and lush meadows. There was a huge bed with brass knobs, plenty of drawers, and two wardrobes. A door led through into a tiny bathroom with a sea-green bath and a cork-tiled floor.

The view, though, held her attention. It was the same scene as from the downstairs window, except that she could see more. The smooth courtyard below, the colourful gardens, open heath that stretched as far as the sea itself, dotted here and there with sheep, flushed with colourful wild flowers. There was a hint of the ruggedness of the cliffs, but she guessed that not until you were on top of them would you experience how dangerous they were.

The sea danced in the light from the sun, scintillating, tempting, and entirely captivating. To Gisele, who had lived in a town all her life, it spelt freedom. She felt that here she could be as close to nature as it was possible to be.

She forgot the time, she forgot everything except the beauty of the scene before her eyes. Far away on the horizon a sweep of purple suggested that there was an island out there, nearer at hand a speedboat cut through the water, leaving a startlingly clear wake of white foam.

Then Nathaniel's voice boomed up the stairs and she was startled out of her daydream. 'Coming!' she called, realising that she had not yet washed or changed.

Frantically she splashed water on her face, exchanged her skirt and blouse for the first dress she came to in her case, dragged a brush through her protesting hair, then tried to appear calm and poised as she walked into the dining room.

Catherine sat at the table, her brother hovering beside her, his immense height making the woman look even tinier and more delicate than before. She laughed when she saw Gisele's flushed face. 'There was no need to rush. You shouldn't take any notice of Nat. Let me guess, you were admiring the view and forgot the time?'

Gisele nodded self-consciously, trying to ignore Nathaniel's dark frown. 'It's superb. I'm so used to looking out at nothing but buildings that I can't get over it. The sea's fascinating. Is it safe to swim?'

'You must never attempt to get down those cliffs,' snarled Nathaniel immediately. 'One slip and you'll end up in pieces on the rocks. Don't ever go near them.'

'Unfortunately that's true,' nodded his sister. 'But there are beaches not too far away. The Atlantic's rollers are ideal for surfing, if you enjoy that sort of thing, or on the other side of the headland, in the Camel Estuary, it's calm enough for even a novice.'

'The Atlantic's mighty powerful, and exceedingly dangerous for the unwary,' said Nathaniel firmly. 'I think that if Gisele wants to swim she should use the pool, unless I'm with her.'

Gisele lifted her brows, and seeing this Catherine

said, 'Didn't he tell you about the pool? Didn't he tell you *anything*?' Her husky laugh was music in the room. 'Shame on you, Nat! How could you bring her here and not tell her what to expect?'

'We had other things to discuss.' He looked at Gisele darkly, his eyes smouldering, and he made it sound as though they had been so full of themselves that they had no time for anything else.

Wouldn't Catherine be surprised, thought Gisele, if she knew they had hardly spoken for the entire journey? That there had been an atmosphere so thick you could cut it with a knife.

'How lovely!' laughed Catherine. 'I'd forgotten what it's like to be young and in love.' A shadow flitted across her face, gone almost instantly, but Gisele knew she recalled the young man who had treated her so shabbily.

'You think twenty-five is old?' mocked her brother lightly. 'Who knows, one of these days a knight on a white charger might come along and sweep you off your feet!'

'Physically, you mean?' tossed Catherine, bubbling with mirth.

'God, I'm sorry,' he said quickly. 'Catherine, you're so damned matter-of-fact about it all, I never think.'

'I don't want you to,' she returned. 'I want to be treated as normal, when are you going to realise that?'

A shuddering sigh shook his big frame. 'I don't think I ever will. It's my fault you're like this, I——'

'Gisele, shut him up, will you?' interjected Catherine. 'Give him a kiss, for goodness' sake. Give him something else to think about!'

Gisele eyed him and knew she could not comply with this pretty woman's request. Nathaniel, though, had no such qualms. In two strides he was across the room, his powerful arms wrapped tightly about her waist. If she did not want her head buried in his chest she had no choice but to lift it. His mouth was waiting, his smoky eyes daring her to repulse him.

It was a brief though infinitely tender kiss. The exciting male smell of him teased Gisele's nostrils and incited her mind. When Nathaniel put her from him she was trembling. He quirked an amused black brow as he looked down at her, and it was not difficult to guess what he thought.

'We'll eat now, shall we?' he suggested softly, 'or have you, like me, food of a different kind at the forefront of your mind?'

She wanted to deny it hotly, but his sister was listening with interest. 'Maybe,' she teased, laughing up into his face, her green eyes wide. 'I'm giving nothing away.'

But her racing pulses gave away the fact that she was not as immune to him as she would like to be. It was disconcerting to discover how easily he could arouse her. What had happened to her good intentions? Why was she weakening?

'That's right,' laughed Catherine. 'Keep 'em waiting, is my motto! I love Nat as a brother, but I wouldn't like him for a boy-friend. He's far too superior. He thinks he's God's gift to women. Why wasn't he born with a hooked nose and cross eyes?'

'And then we would neither of us have met the delightful Gisele,' he threw back lightly. 'Isn't she quite the most beautiful woman you've ever seen?'

Gisele flushed under his scrutiny, sitting quickly, tensing when she felt his hands on her shoulders. She was beginning to realise that it wouldn't be too much of a problem pretending to love Nat. He excited her, despite all her efforts to remain cool.

'You're embarrassing her,' said Catherine. 'But I agree, all the same. I have a feeling we're going to be firm friends.'

Nathaniel smiled, satisfied, and slid into his own chair. 'I'm starving. Ring your bell, Catherine, let Meg know we're ready.'

But as though on cue the plump, motherly figure of the housekeeper came into the room, carrying a loaded tray which she set down on a side table.

She had grey hair curling about a round face. Button-bright eyes looked at Gisele curiously and Nathaniel said, 'Meg, this is Gisele, my fiancée. Gisele—Meg, our treasure. She's a retired nurse, used to live in Padstow, but now looks after Catherine and the house, and does everything that anyone asks of her quite willingly and cheerfully, and I don't know what we'd do without her.'

'Get away with you, Nat!' scolded the older woman, but she looked pleased all the same, and as she ladled home-made tomato soup into their dishes Gisele noticed that she gave Nathaniel an extra big helping. He was clearly as much as favourite with her as she was with him.

Catherine drank her soup slowly and carefully, each spoonful lifted to her mouth with a determined effort to spill none.

Nathaniel looked at her incredulously. 'Your hands, Catherine! You're using your hands!'

She laughed delightedly. 'My surprise! The use is coming back. Isn't that wonderful?'

'It's truly amazing. How long's this been happening? Why didn't you tell me?'

'Because it's taken a long time,' she said simply, 'and a lot of determination.'

For the rest of the meal he could not take his eyes off her, clearly unable to believe that his sister's condition was improving. Gisele wondered whether it meant she wouldn't be needed.

Afterwards Nathaniel suggested she might like to

unpack, but it was a slow job because repeatedly she was drawn towards the window, the sea with its constantly changing surface luring her like a moth to a flame. She could not wait to explore.

When she eventually went back downstairs Catherine was alone. 'Nat's gone for a walk,' she told Gisele.

'Oh!' Gisele's disappointment shadowed her face.

'You would like to go too?' asked Catherine quickly. 'I thought you might, but he said you'd be tired. Why don't you go after him? He's been gone no more than a minute.'

'Would you mind?'

'Of course not,' returned his sister. 'Look, there he is, out on the headland. Hurry, Gisele!'

She needed no further urging. Her feet flew across the springy turf. She inhaled deeply and smelt heather and the sea, and the sun, and all that was good and fresh in this delightful place.

After every few steps she stopped and looked about her. Golden flowers dusted the hillside, sea thrift and sea lavender bathed other slopes in a mist of pink and purple. She felt as though she were walking through Paradise.

Nathaniel was no longer in sight, but she knew the general direction he had taken, and because Catherine was sure to be watching she walked the same path. But she did not try to catch him up. He might not want her. For what other reason would he go alone? Besides, there was so much to see, so many different flowers to stop and inspect. She could taste salt in the air, dozens of seabirds screamed and called. It was heaven.

She had walked right to the edge of the cliff before she saw Nathaniel. Daring to look over, catching her breath at the sheer drop, she involuntarily clapped a hand to her mouth when she saw him right beneath her, climbing down with the surefootedness of a mountain goat.

He had warned her how dangerous they were. Why then was he risking his own life? One false move and it could be he who was smashed to pieces at the bottom. It was a long way, with little or nothing to break his fall if he should slip.

Nathaniel, be careful! she implored silently, knowing that if he heard her voice he would look up and maybe lose his footing as a result. But almost as if she had spoken the words aloud he raised his eyes. She sensed rather than saw the tensing of him.

'Get back!' he shouted sharply, angrily. 'You're too near the edge!'

His voice was carried to her in the same breeze that lifted her hair and sprayed the ocean into her face. The tide was coming in fast and she could see for herself those dangerous Atlantic rollers—giant, white-crested waves that reached for the shoreline, meeting the rocks with a boom that sounded like thunder, sending up fairytale plumes of spray.

'What are you doing?' she screamed, then realised that her voice was being blown back. Only a seagull echoed in response. The wind here was much stronger than near the house.

'Gisele, go back!' Nathaniel commanded again. And then a new sound reached her ears, a plaintive bleating! She scanned the cliffs below Nathaniel, but saw nothing. Perhaps she was mistaken? Without thinking she took a step nearer, then screamed as the ground crumbled beneath her foot.

Instinctively she threw herself backwards, her heart pounding, prickly heat bathing her skin, her arms flailing the air.

She heard a shower of stones course down the

cliffside, gathering momentum as they fell. And then Nathaniel's muffled curse as they rained on his body before pursuing their relentless course.

'*Gisele!*' His angry voice reached her yet again.

It could all have taken no more than a few seconds, but to Gisele it seemed eternity. On her stomach now, she edged forward and peered down. 'I'm all right,' she called, but whether he heard was debatable.

'Go home!' he boomed, with a power that matched the waves.

She risked another few inches and cupped her hands round her mouth. 'What are you doing?'

'What the hell's it look like? There's a lamb stuck. I must get him.'

'Be careful!' she yelled. 'It's not worth your own life!'

'I'm in no danger—only from you. For God's sake, *move!*' This last word reverberated back from the cliffs, startling gulls and kittiwakes into flight, and the lamb into an even more frantic bleating.

Gisele wriggled out of sight, but she was not going to return to the house knowing that Nathaniel had only to make one false move and he could kill himself. If he needed help she must be there to hear his call.

The next half hour was the longest she had ever spent. Constantly she heard the sound of stones skittering down the cliff face, each time she held her breath fearing Nathaniel's fall might come next.

Then the lamb's plaintive cry changed to one of pain, and she risked another look over the edge. At first she could see neither, then she spotted Nathaniel's broad back bent over the animal. They were on a narrow ledge beneath a jutting rock.

How the lamb had got there was beyond her, but more worrying, how was Nathaniel going to get back? He would need to swing himself out and up, there was no foothold to climb sideways. With the lamb in his arms it would be impossible. He had been a fool to go down.

'Gisele!' His voice reached her, even though she knew he could not see her. 'Are you still there?'

'Yes, Nathaniel,' she called through cupped hands.

'Go and fetch a rope, a long rope, do you hear that?'

'I hear you,' she replied. 'What are you going to do?'

'The lamb's broken its leg, he won't let me lift him. Bring two pieces of wood as well, for splints. I'll bandage his leg and then truss him. You'll have to haul him up. Think you can manage it?'

A shudder of fear jerked through her. 'Me?' she squeaked. What if he was too heavy? What if she let him go? What if he pulled her over? Oh, God! Didn't Nathaniel realise what he was asking?

'Gisele!' he roared.

She swallowed, her mouth dry, her heart crashing against her ribs, echoing in her ears. 'I'll try, but I might not be strong enough. Isn't there——'

He cut her off impatiently. 'Don't argue! Get going, woman, *now*!'

After one last fearful glance Gisele turned and ran, stumbling and falling in her haste. She reached Stormhaven breathless and dishevelled and found Meg in the kitchen.

'My dear body and soul!' cried the woman. 'Whatever's the matter? Sit yourself down and catch your breath. You look as though you've been frightened half out of your wits!'

'It's Nathaniel,' panted Gisele urgently. 'He's down the cliff—after a lamb. He wants a rope—and some splints. He wants me to—pull the lamb up." Each short sentence was punctuated with deep gulping breaths.

'Mercy me!' Meg pushed up her sleeves. 'I thought he was too old for tricks like that. I'll come with you, m'dear. There's some rope in the garage, and we'll pick up some sticks on our way.'

Once Meg had taken over Gisele was able to think more clearly. She spotted a first-aid tin in the kitchen and grabbed a roll of bandage, which she popped into a plastic bag that was lying on the table, tying it to the end of the rope as they made their urgent way across the headland.

Meg's age and weight were against her, and Gisele had reached the cliff edge and thrown down the rope before she caught up.

They stood and waited anxiously, holding their end of the rope between them. The lamb's cries rose as Nathaniel applied the splints, and the rope jerked as he struggled to fasten it around the animal.

'Pull now!' he roared. 'Slowly. I'll climb behind and steady the little fellow.'

Gisele would never have managed on her own. She realised that the moment they began to haul up their strange burden. The lamb was a dead weight and it took all her strength as well as Meg's to pull him to the top.

The pathetic grey bundle made its appearance at the same time as the familiar black hair of Nathaniel. Gisele never took her eyes off Nat as he hauled himself over the edge, then her lids closed and she shivered, realising that despite the heat of the sun and her physical exertion she was stone cold. He could have got himself killed, and much as she hated him she did not want that to happen.

'Twuz nibby jibby, sure nuff,' said Meg, her face flushed, her ample bosom heaving.

Gisele's eyes shot wide. 'What did you say?'

Nathaniel laughed, seeming none the worse for wear

after his climb. 'A close shave, that's what she meant. You'll get used to Meg's Cornish sayings.'

He dropped to his knees and untied the rope from round the hapless lamb. The animal was exhausted, its bleat growing weaker, no longer attempting to struggle.

'Does this happen often?' asked Gisele, wondering if he had taken such risks before because of these stupid animals.

He shook his head. 'Very rarely. They've usually got more sense. This one's a bit young—a late comer. He must have wandered from his mother. I'll take him back to the house and have a look at his leg. Are you fit?'

Not as fit as he was, by the look of him. Perspiration beaded his brow, but his breathing was normal. No one would ever guess he had just climbed a hundred feet or more up a cliff face. He had to be in perfect physical condition.

Gisele followed as he strode across the heath, the lamb cradled in his arms. Her legs felt shaky, and Meg, too, was having difficulty catching her breath.

Nathaniel's shirt clung wetly to his back, emphasising powerful muscles, drawing her attention to his lean masculinity. He had a long loose stride, an easy movement that was sensual to look at.

Gisele watched him closely, liking the way the sun made his hair shine blue-black, admiring the strong curve of his neck as he bent his head over the lamb, the width of shoulder, the tightly-muscled thighs that flexed against his denims with each step.

There was nothing weak about Nathaniel. He was a man to surpass all men, risking his own life to save one pitiful lamb, giving no heed at all to his own safety, conscious only that a creature was in distress.

There were so many facets to his nature that she

wondered whether she would get to know them all before her time here was finished. And oddly, she wanted to find out more about this man.

Catherine waited anxiously in the yard. 'I saw you all rushing about. What's happened? I thought it was you, Nat. Why didn't someone tell me? Oh!' She spotted the lamb. 'The poor thing! Give it to me.'

Smiling fondly, Nathaniel gently lowered his burden on to his sister's lap. 'He fell over the cliff,' he told her.

'And you went down?' she scolded angrily. 'Typical! What if you'd fallen? Gisele must have been out of her mind!'

He switched his attention. 'Were you, Gisele?' Humour lurked in his eyes, an unspoken question.

Gisele felt her pulse miss and then race beneath that dark gaze. 'But of course, darling.' There was a quiver in her voice as she spoke the unaccustomed endearment—and she had felt worried, but no more so than she would for any other person who risked their life, she hastened to assure herself.

'There, you see?' cried Catherine. 'She's quite overcome. Meg, be an angel and make us a pot of strong tea.'

The woman bustled into the house, Nathaniel pushing his sister's wheelchair, Gisele bringing up the rear.

They went into the kitchen and he picked up the lamb, depositing it on the table, much to the housekeeper's disgust. He took off the bandages and gently manipulated the injured leg until he was satisfied, applying a clean bandage dipped into a mixture of plaster of Paris. The animal was unconscious by this time.

'He'll do,' said Nathaniel at length. 'The plaster will have set by the time he comes round.'

Gisele had watched fascinated throughout the whole operation. 'How did you know what to do?' she queried.

He grinned. 'I used to help the local vet when I was a kid. I thought I might become a veterinary surgeon myself, but it went the way all other grand ideas children have.'

She was impressed nevertheless.

They drank several cups of hot tea, and then the lamb regained consciousness and Meg made a fuss of him. She fixed a corner in the kitchen for him to rest, cleaned the table with plenty of disinfectant and ushered them all out.

'He'll be spoilt something rotten now,' said Nathaniel to no one in particular, and then to Gisele, 'I'd like a word with you, if you'll excuse us, Catherine?'

His sister's fine brows rose. 'Don't mind me, you two lovebirds. I quite understand.'

'I was going to take a shower and change,' said Gisele, wondering what he wanted to say that couldn't be said in front of Catherine. 'Won't it wait?'

'I'm afraid not,' he said brusquely. 'Your room will do. I shan't keep you long.'

It was clear to her, if not to his sister, that a cuddle and a kiss were the furthest thoughts from his mind. He looked cross all of a sudden, and out of sorts, and she felt a shiver of apprehension.

He followed her closely into her room, shutting the door and leaning back against it. Some of the sunshine faded, a dark cloud loomed on the horizon.

'Don't ever do that again!' Thick black brows jutted uncompromisingly above narrowed eyes. His lips thinned so as to be almost invisible, and a telltale muscle jerked spasmodically in his jaw.

His hands were thrust into his trouser pockets, and

she could only guess that his fingers might be curled, that whatever was annoying him, he was exercising great restraint in keeping his hands off her.

Gisele eyed him hostilely. 'Suppose you tell me what it is I've done?' Her head was tilted slightly to one side, the light from the window setting fire to her hair, her fingers linked demurely in front of her.

'Going so near to the cliff-edge that you almost fell! Haven't you more sense? Why didn't you heed my earlier warning?'

She felt like a schoolgirl being chastised by her teacher, but she had no intention of meekly taking it. '*You* went down. I was concerned for *your* safety, not mine.'

'I hardly think so,' he said coldly. 'We both know what you think of me—the type of man I am. Good riddance, you'd probably say.'

'Maybe I would,' she returned bitterly. 'Maybe I should have given you a helping hand.'

'Sounds more logical,' he snarled, pushing himself away from the door and striding over to the window. His shoulders were tense as he looked out across the rolling heath, making Gisele wonder what thoughts really were going through his mind.

'Is that all you wanted?' she asked tightly. 'If so, you can go. I'm filthy and exhausted and I'd like a wash and a rest, if you wouldn't mind?'

Nathaniel turned slowly, and this time the sunlight caught his hair, outlining the springy curls with a thread of silver, throwing his face into shadow, emphasising the height and breadth of him like nothing else could.

He was like a supreme being, he towered above all. A giant of a man whose word in this house was law. And he did not take kindly to having his orders disobeyed.

'I want you to promise me, Gisele, that you'll never go near those cliffs again.'

'Why should I?' she returned hotly. It was difficult to read his expression with the sunlight directly in her face. 'I'm not a child. I think I'm capable of making such a decision for myself, without you dictating what I should or should not do!.

He drew in a sharp hissing breath. 'Don't try my patience, Gisele, just promise, then I'll go.'

She shook her head, red hair flying, eyes flashing. 'I don't have to promise you anything. Credit me with some sense, that's all I ask.'

'Hell, you're so pigheaded,' he gritted. 'Is it such a big thing I'm asking? Don't you realise that I'm responsible for you being here, that if anything should happen I——' A shudder ran through his frame.

'Would be to blame?' she suggested sweetly. 'That's right, you would, wouldn't you? But don't worry, I have no intention of taking my own life. Unless, of course, you make it entirely intolerable for me here. The way you're going on anything could happen—a girl can only take so much.'

'So too can I.' His breathing had noticeably deepened. 'And you know very well that I didn't mean I was afraid of you deliberately throwing yourself off the cliff. Accidents happen—you proved that when you slipped.'

Again he walked across the room, moving lightly and silently for so big a man. He could creep up on you in the dark and you wouldn't even know, thought Gisele.

'I think,' she said impatiently, 'you're making a lot of fuss about nothing. Maybe I am an ignorant townie, but I'm not stupid enough to make the same mistake twice. I accept that your cliffs are dangerous. Is that what you want?'

One half of her was seething over his treatment, the other responded with alarming vibrancy to his compelling masculinity. His face was harsh, cheekbones jutting angularly, jaw thrust forward with an aggression that was as exciting as it was irritating.

He was the typical male she despised, yet amazingly her physical awareness threatened to engulf all other feelings. Right at this moment he felt nothing more for her than contempt, he was annoyed because she had almost slipped and it could have looked bad for him, yet even so her body craved contact.

It was sheer lunacy. From the first moment she had seen him—no, from the time she had heard his voice, there had been an instant response. And do what she liked, feel about him as she liked, she could no more dismiss him than she could a raging toothache.

He gnawed insidiously at her nerve-ends, encroaching slowly, inch by slow inch, until one day she would be unable to do anything about it. One look into that strong sensual face and her limbs turned to water. He was a perfect specimen of irresistible virility.

'I expect it will have to do.' His voice was dry, scarcely tolerant.

Gisele looked at him, venting her feelings in anger. 'It's the best you're getting, *Mr* Oakley. Now would you mind leaving? I'm really getting very tired of standing around waiting for you to go.'

'And you're making things very difficult for me,' he shot angrily. 'Why the hell do you have to react like this when I'm trying to talk reasonably?'

She shrugged. 'Probably because I don't think it reasonable. I resent you speaking to me so peremptorily, if you must know. I'm here to do you a favour, although it looks as if I might not be needed, and I can't say I'm sorry. But it might help if you were nice to me instead of constantly at my throat. It's not going to make a very pleasant atmosphere when we join your sister. What's she going to think when she realises we've been arguing?'

'She needn't know.' His face darkened with displeasure.

'Perhaps you're a good actor, but I'm not,' she flung at him. 'You should have thought about that before deciding to chastise me!'

Nathaniel moved closer and took her shoulders before she realised what he was doing. 'That wasn't my intention.'

'Then what was?' Gisele lifted her chin and held his gaze, noting how very tiny his pupils were in the strong sunlight. It made his eyes look lighter, more menacing, and she could not contain a quiver, though whether it was apprehension or anticipation she dared not hazard a guess.

She could feel every finger digging into the fleshless bones of her shoulders, and they sent shock-waves through her system as though each one was charged with electricity.

'Would it be too much for you to accept that I might be concerned about you, as a person, not simply as a girl here to do a job?'

She looked at him coldly. 'Yes, Nathaniel, I'm afraid it would. You don't care about people—your sister excepted, of course. You get through girls like anyone else does hot dinners. They mean nothing to you. *Nothing!*' She flung this last word contemptuously.

It exhilarated her to see the exasperation in his face. It was a dangerous game, taunting Nathaniel, but the sheer nearness of him, his overpowering maleness, sent her senses reeling and her mind eddying, until she did not know what she was doing.

'You're right,' he said surprisingly. 'I've never yet met a girl worthy of my love.'

Gisele laughed, she could not help it. 'Listen to you, the original male chauvinist! Whatever gave you that idea?'

The darkening of his brow should have warned her, the treacherous tightening of his jaw, the increasing pressure in his fingertips. But she went on blithely, 'What an inflated opinion you have of yourself! It makes me wonder whether it isn't the girls who reject you, not the other way round. Am I mistaken, Mr *Lothario*, sir?'

For a full five seconds they stared at each other, Nathaniel looking as though he would like nothing better than to slap her, then with a groan he pulled her savagely into his arms.

CHAPTER SEVEN

THERE was no escaping Nathaniel's kiss. Gisele found herself responding even before she realised what she was doing. It was a purely automatic reaction.

He crushed her to him, moulding her against his hard bones so that the heat from him penetrated through the flimsy material of her dress. The intoxicating male smell of him sent her senses reeling until she was incapable of coherent thought.

His lips bruised hers relentlessly, forcing her own apart. Time had no meaning, and Gisele was soon lost in a world of spinning senses, and excitement that shot flames through her nerve-streams and carried her along in a vortex of emotions and desire.

When he abruptly put her from him she felt bereft. Why had he stopped when for once she had forgotten herself sufficiently to respond?

'Now we both know,' he snapped. 'You're not really the cold little fish you purport to be!'

His derision cut through her like a knife, bringing her back to her senses with a jolt. She ought to have known he was testing her. He had chosen his moment with uncanny accuracy, and she would never forgive him for it, never!

'I wasn't aware that my feelings were in question?' Her tone was as cutting as his.

'Very much so,' he thrust tightly. 'Whether Catherine needs you or not we still have to convince her that we're in love.'

Gisele tossed her head scornfully, her red hair a vivid flame of fire. 'You should have thought of that before you tore me off a strip. I don't take kindly to being treated like a fool!'

His jaw tensed and he looked at her coldly, dark eyes fixed on her with fierce concentration, as if willing her to change her attitude. He really knew very little about the female sex if he thought he could treat her like this and still expect her to be loving in front of his sister.

'Why don't you say what you're thinking?' she goaded. 'I have a feeling you'd like to get your fingers round my neck and squeeze the life out of me!'

'Too true, I would,' he gritted. 'You're the most infuriating woman I've ever met!'

'I think the same could be said of you,' Gisele returned evenly, lifting her brows and staring at him with wide luminous eyes. 'So where does that leave us? Two people constantly rubbing each other up the wrong way, yet forced to pretend a love we don't feel. Were you afraid you'd spoil your image by confessing I was anything less than an intimate friend?'

'For pity's sake, Gisele, stow it!' he grated harshly, a muscle working in his jaw. 'We both know the reason I claimed you were my fiancée—and it certainly isn't the one you're making out.'

'Oh, wasn't it? I'm sorry,' she said with affected innocence.

He expelled his breath furiously and swung away, wrenching open the door and stepping through it without a backward glance. Gisele tensed herself as she waited for it to bang and was taken by surprise when he closed it quietly. Then she realised that, of course, Catherine would hear and want to know what it was all about. And he would not be able to find an answer for that!

She wished she had never agreed to come. Catherine was a darling, and she liked her a lot and would love to help in any way she could, but not at the expense of having her nerves constantly shattered by her irritating brother.

He seemed to think that he had the right to dictate, that because she was employed by him he could give his orders. It seemed to have escaped him that she was a human being, with all the feelings that go with it, and she liked to be treated with respect, if nothing else.

She tore off her clothes with trembling fingers and stepped beneath the shower, allowing the needle-fine jets of water to cool her overheated body and calm her seething temper.

Squirting liquid soap into her palm, she lathered herself all over, aware that only seconds earlier these very same limbs had pulsed with desire, that she had craved fulfilment from Nathaniel.

She must have been insane—and yet, even as the thought crossed her mind, she wondered what it would feel like to have his hands sliding over her like this, exploring each and every curve, his lips following the line of his hands.

Almost as though he were actually touching her, she quivered and felt desire begin to rise from the pit of her stomach. Feelings she had kept suppressed for so long struggled to the surface—and she slammed them down quickly.

It was madness. Nathaniel's only motive for kissing her was to convince his sister they were in love. He was using her shamelessly to suit his own ends. But he was such an expert that he was managing to inject life into her deliberately deep-frozen emotions.

She must never let herself respond again. Once back in London she would mean no more to him than any other girl of his acquaintance. They were like ships that pass in the night—forgotten the next day as though they had never been.

With fury now she scrubbed her skin, trying to erase the feel of him from it, trying to wash him out of her mind for ever. She turned the jets to cold and did not step out until she was shivering from head to toe.

Then she towelled herself briskly until her body glowed. She glanced at her watch on the dressing table, shocked to see how late it was. She had hoped to rest before dinner, but the incident over the lamb and her quarrel with Nathaniel had taken up more time than she realised.

It did not seem important what she wore, but in deference to Catherine she chose a pretty lemon blouse with a darker yellow skirt. The skirt clung sensually to her hips, emphasising her curves, moving with her as she walked.

She had not worn it for a long time and must have put on weight. Not that it mattered, it was not ridiculously tight, but she doubted whether the fact would go unnoticed by Nathaniel.

Her hair was more of a problem. She attacked it furiously with brush and comb, but no matter what she did it insisted on going its own way. In the end she gave up, dragging it severely back and fastening it with a band. It was an unbecoming style, but at least it was out of the way.

As at lunchtime Nathaniel and his sister were in the dining room waiting. It was a pleasant room, high-ceilinged and elegant with Regency furniture, the décor in toning shades of green. It was cool and peaceful, and Gisele felt herself relaxing.

Catherine sat in her wheelchair, Nathaniel standing beside her with a glass of amber liquid in his hand. He smiled warmly when Gisele entered, no trace on his handsome face of the aggression he had shown earlier.

He looked devastating in cream shirt and dark brown trousers, the shirt open to reveal the strong column of his throat, allowing a glimpse of dark hairs covering his hard-muscled chest. His black hair was still damp, waving closely to his head, emphasising the fine shape of it, the high proud brow, the aristocratic nose.

'A drink, Gisele?' he suggested softly, moving towards her, his feet soundless on the smooth velvet-piled carpet. For the moment he blocked Catherine from her view. He took her hand and the warning pressure, coupled with signals from his eyes, told her she had best behave, or else!

'A small sherry, please,' she said, eyeing him warily, ashamed to feel yet again an unwitting response to his touch.

His hand moved to her waist before sliding over the curve of her hip. 'Mmm, nice,' he murmured. 'You feel as good as you look. Should I flatter myself that you've dressed to please me?'

'But who else?' she parried lightly. His clean fresh smell reminded her of the heather and the sea, and she smiled, quite involuntarily, and was rewarded with a kiss that set her pulses racing and brought a delicate flush to her cheeks.

Why couldn't he always be this nice, then she would have no difficulty in playing the part he had given her. She pushed him away gently, feeling the heat of his body beneath her palm—and a vibrant tingle ran through her!

He moved, a smile gentling his lips, satisfied for the moment that she would not let him down. Gisele looked at Catherine, who had been unashamedly watching. 'You'll have to forgive us—I think Nat sometimes forgets we're not alone.'

'For pity's sake don't worry about me,' Catherine trilled. 'I'm pleased to see you both so happy and so very much in love. Tell me, where are you going to live when you're married? I'd like to think you'll make Stormhaven your home.'

Gisele looked quickly across at Nathaniel, but he was busy pouring her drink and appeared not to have heard. She shrugged and coloured furiously. 'I don't really know. But with Nathaniel's work in London, I suppose he'll—we'll—live there.'

He came across and handed her her sherry. 'That's right. But it's far too soon to be thinking about anything like that.'

So he had heard! Gisele darted him a furious glance. Why hadn't he answered instead of letting her make a mess of it?

'I don't see why,' said Catherine in surprise. 'You're in love, and you're engaged, which must mean you're serious, so why wait?' She gave him a teasing smile. 'And you're not getting any younger, dear brother of mine.'

'Thirty-three isn't old!' he returned with pretended indignation. 'I've not yet reached my prime.'

'Well, I don't think you should wait,' said Catherine firmly. 'I want you to make up your mind before you leave here exactly when the wedding is to be. You will get married at St Petroc's, of course? You're not going to make me go all the way to London?'

Gisele held her breath, waiting for Nathaniel's reply. How was he going to get out of that one without giving the game away?

He rested his hand on her shoulder and she moved towards him, unconsciously seeking reassurance. '*When* I get married, Catherine my sweet, it will most certainly be at St Petroc's, you can rest assured about that. But when it will be depends entirely on——'

He looked down at Gisele, his eyes full of wicked humour, and she felt shocked to the core. He was going to put the onus on her! He was trapping her!

What game was he playing? Her eyes locked into his, her body rigid.

'On when I can spare the time away from my work,' he finished calmly.

Relief washed over Gisele and she drew a deep rasping, shuddering breath, filling her stifled lungs with desperately needed air, her legs so weak that had he not held her she would have collapsed.

'Nathaniel!' exclaimed Catherine sharply, shock making her voice unusually sharp. 'How can you be so callous? Look what you've done to poor Gisele!' She shot her chair towards them, her blue eyes flashing angrily. 'Now say you're sorry. If you won't fix it up I'll do it for you. Heavens, Gisele must think you don't want to marry her? What type of a man are you, to put his work before his future bride?'

His thick brows rose and disappeared into his hair which, as it dried, had fallen across his forehead. 'I'm already taking a holiday, Catherine,' he said gently. 'I may be the boss, but I believe in setting a good example.'

'And how about Gisele? Have you asked her if she minds waiting?'

His eyes flicked to the redhead at his side. 'Gisele does as she's told.'

Catherine shook her head disbelievingly. 'How can you, my own brother, say that? We women are liberated now, we're allowed a say in what goes on. You're living in the wrong decade if you think you can dictate to her!'

She looked at Gisele, her pretty face flushed. 'Tell him! I'm sure *you* must want to get married soon. What's the point in waiting?'

Gisele did not know what to say. The whole conversation was escalating out of all proportion. She lifted her shoulders and looked helpless. 'I'm in

Nathaniel's hands,' she said softly, attempting to imply that she was so hopelessly captivated by him that whatever he said went.

Catherine's eyes sparked from one to the other. 'You're fools, both of you. Who knows what life holds in store? Snatch your happiness while you can.'

There was a break in her voice and she whirled her chair round so that they should not see her face. The next second she was as composed as ever. 'I'm sorry, it's nothing to do with me. Shall we have dinner?'

It was very clear what thoughts had been going through her mind. Gisele looked at Nathaniel and saw the whiteness round his mouth. He had needed no reminding that it was his fault his sister was not now happily married.

She slid her arm about his waist, feeling a need to comfort him, but he pulled away abruptly and took his seat at the table.

Dinner was an uncomfortable meal after that. They talked and laughed, Catherine making the biggest effort of all, but it was superficial, and Gisele was glad when it was over.

Nathaniel went with his sister into the room with the view and Gisele decided to go for a walk. It was a still, warm evening, the wind that had been blowing earlier having died completely away.

The gardens were a blaze of roses in small raised beds between smooth concrete paths. A row of tamarisk protected them, their graceful feathery fronds an effective foil for the brilliant flowers.

Gisele heard the sound of running water and through a rustic arch, covered with more huge sweetly-scented roses, discovered a tiny natural stream. It was no more than a trickle, yet it had been expertly landscaped into the garden, every advantage being taken of its meandering course.

There were no flowers here, foliage plants being used instead with unique effect. There was a tiny arbour sited so as to obtain the best view of this delightful water garden, and Gisele sat down. She thought it must be the most peaceful place on earth.

She closed her eyes and listened to the different sounds. Predominant was the trickling of water, but also came the whirr of insects' wings, the drone of bees, the incessant screaming of gulls, and the occasional faraway bleat of a lamb.

When footsteps joined the sounds she knew she was about to have company, and she resented the thought of Nathaniel spoiling these few quiet moments.

'So there you are!' His deep-timbred voice reached her before she saw him, and when he appeared her heart pounded traitorously.

But her tones were perfectly cool. 'I was looking forward to a few minutes on my own. Did you have to ruin it?'

He shrugged. 'It was Catherine's suggestion. She seems to think she may have caused a certain amount of dissension between us. She sent me to kiss and make up.'

Gisele tossed her head arrogantly.

His lips quirked and there was definite amusement in his dark eyes. 'I take it the idea doesn't appeal? Pity! I thought it rather a good one myself.'

He eased himself on to the seat beside her. There was not really room for two and Gisele found herself trapped against him. Contact sent an explosion of feeling through her veins and the blood singing in her ears until she thought her head was going to burst.

'Catherine's told me off for not giving you an engagement ring,' he said. 'It might be as well if we drive into Plymouth tomorrow and put the matter in order.'

No other woman would be allowed to dictate to him, thought Gisele. Catherine could get away with murder. But—*put the matter in order!* He made it sound like a business transaction. Her chin jutted angrily. 'There's no need. It would be a waste of money.'

'I can afford it.'

She sensed his disapproval of her attitude. 'I've no doubt you can, but why throw it away? Or were you perhaps contemplating giving the ring to the next in line? It could be useful to have one at the ready just in case.'

His head whipped round and the dark anger in his eyes made her flinch. 'Do you enjoy being rude, Miss Latham?'

Did she? Now she came to think of it, it did give her a curious elation. Goading Nathaniel was a heady thing. Perhaps she did enjoy it. She had certainly never spoken to anyone else in this manner.

She arched her perfectly shaped brows, her beautiful eyes an echo of the greenery surrounding them. 'Miss Latham now, is it? Oh dear, *Mr* Oakley, I wonder what Catherine will have to say about this? Seems like we're regressing instead of moving on!'

'Damn you!' he snarled, his fingers curling tightly over the edge of the seat, knuckles gleaming. 'I'll make you pay for this. No one speaks to me in that tone and gets away with it!'

'No one—up till now, that is,' she returned sweetly. 'If you don't like the way I am why didn't you use one of your little yes-girls to play the part?'

'Because, dammit, they wouldn't—hell, why should I explain myself to you?' His eyes bore into her like red-hot pokers and Gisele shrank away. Spiky branches dug into her skin, but she would rather suffer than sit any closer to this objectionable man.

She eyed him coldly. 'You've no need to explain—it's perfectly clear. They wouldn't suit Catherine. They could no more be friends with her than with——' She searched for a simile and failed.

'On the other hand, they would be exactly the sort of diversion you're looking for, someone ready to fall into your bed at the drop of a hat. I expect it's hell not having anyone to satisfy your—er—natural urges? Isn't it a pity you couldn't have found someone who would give you the best of both worlds?'

She expected him to retaliate, but strangely he sat still and as silent as a statue, only his irregular breathing giving away the fact that he was not as calm as he looked.

As the silence between them lengthened Gisele began to feel uneasy. It was no fun baiting him if he refused to be drawn. It made her feel stupid and childish and could only do harm so far as Catherine was concerned. Besides. she didn't want to be his enemy.

Nervously she twisted her fingers in her lap. 'I'm sorry,' and when he did not answer, 'I had no right saying that. I didn't mean it. It was just that you made me so mad I couldn't help myself.'

'I see,' he said tightly at length. 'And did you think that apologising is going to put it right? That I shall forget your nasty insinuations and we'll form a nice cosy twosome, so that neither Catherine nor anyone else will ever suspect what a perfect little bitch you are?'

Gisele gasped. Surely she hadn't asked for that? Their eyes met and locked in silent battle, and it seemed a lifetime before Nathaniel finally relaxed and pushed himself up.

She rose too, standing close to him. 'Now what?' he snarled, looking down at her coldly. 'If you think my sister was right and we should kiss and make up after all, don't count on it. The idea doesn't appeal to me any more.'

Gisele felt choked inside. She had swallowed her pride and apologised for nothing. Grimly she clenched her teeth and walked away, unaware that he was following until his hand fell heavily on her shoulder and he spun her to face him.

'If it wasn't for Catherine,' he said quietly, and his soft tone was infinitely more threatening than his harsh words, 'I'd take you back to London right now. As it is, her happiness is more important to me than anything else.'

The weight of his hand was like an iron bar, bearing her mercilessly down. 'Perhaps it might be as well if I do go? I'm sure Catherine doesn't really need me—not now she's regaining the use of her hands. I don't see any point in staying.'

'She has a long way to go before she'll be able to write,' snarled Nathaniel. 'Don't think you can back out so easily. In the morning we go to Plymouth for that ring. Right now we're going back to Catherine and you'll behave as though nothing has happened. We're lovers, okay? And you've just been thoroughly and welcomingly kissed.'

Her eyes shot wide, lashes framing them thickly. 'I don't think I can pretend that much.'

'Then we'll have to make sure you get the real thing.' His eyes darkened ominously and the next second his mouth covered hers, his hands moving to the small of her back, guiding her body towards him. Whereas on other occasions his kiss had been ruthless, this time it was carefully calculated to arouse a passion in her that Catherine would be unable to mistake.

His lips brushed hers gently and sensually, sliding over the fullness of her mouth, moving to her chin and her throat, then back against to possess her lips anew.

His hands made their own assault, gliding from her back to her waist, down yet again to her hips, holding her embarrassingly close against his hard masculine body so that she felt every bone and sinew. If he held her any closer they would merge.

Of their own volition her hands, which had at first lain protestingly against his chest, crept over his shoulders, felt the powerful cords in his neck, then mingled with the luxuriant thickness of his hair.

She moulded his head between her palms and held him close, parting her lips so that he could kiss her more deeply, more satisfyingly. He was getting through to her in a way she had never expected, never wanted. But he was like a drug—after the first taste she was addicted.

When he eventually put her from him her body craved for more. Her mouth felt bruised, her limbs weak, and she knew there was a foolish grin on her face.

'I think that should do.' Nathaniel's self-complacency wiped away her smile, but the warmth inside her remained and then he curved his arm about her waist she rested her head against his shoulder. Job or no job, there was something very exciting about being kissed by Nathaniel.

Catherine was suitably convinced, apologising profusely for what she thought had been her own incautious comments about their wedding. 'I really should learn to mind my own business,' she said. 'I hope you've forgiven me?'

Gisele smiled warmly. 'I'd be the same myself, don't worry.' Her hand was linked in Nathaniel's as they sat side by side on the couch. Their truce had resulted in a much easier relationship and she did not even have to pretend. For once she was thoroughly enjoying herself.

When Gisele went to bed that night she felt

exhausted. Never had she spent such a long and eventful day. So much had happened it was incredible there had been enough hours to cram it all in.

She should have slept immediately, yet for some reason she lay wide awake, vividly aware that Nathaniel was sleeping in the next room, that only a few inches of brick wall separated them. She found herself listening, wondering whether he too was having trouble sleeping, or whether he had laid down his head and that was it.

There was no sound to disturb the stillness of the house, so she guessed this must be so. All she could hear was the faint boom of the surf through her open window, and the soft call of a nightjar as it preyed on moths and other flying insects.

Catherine's room was a little farther along the landing. A stairlift had been installed so that she could get upstairs easily and effortlessly, a second wheelchair at her disposal. She had no intention, she said, of sleeping downstairs.

Now she had met Catherine, Gisele was glad she had come, and she hoped she would soon be given the opportunity of helping with her writing. Gradually sleep took over and Gisele knew nothing more until she heard a banging on her door and an impatient voice asking when she was going to get up.

It took a few seconds to gather her senses and recall where she was. Waking up in a strange room and hearing someone yelling was not exactly conducive to coherent thought.

Nathaniel, however, obviously considered she had taken long enough to answer, and he pushed the door roughly open, fixing her with his deep disturbing eyes.

'Get out!' she cried, snatching at the sheets, pulling them right up to her chin. 'I heard you—I'm awake. I'll be down as soon as I'm ready.'

'Do you know what time it is?' he asked abruptly. 'Half past ten. You've slept the clock round.'

And he thought she had no right to sleep in so late! 'I did have a very trying day yesterday,' she said smoothly.

His eyes narrowed. 'And today we're going into Plymouth. Had you forgotten?' He strode into the room, black cords moulding his legs, making them longer and more lethally dangerous. A thin grey sweater hid none of his powerfully muscled chest, merely accentuating each and every movement.

It had escaped her for the moment, now it came back with alarming clarity, that today they were going to choose the ring. Today he was staking his claim properly. So far as any outsiders were concerned she would be his exclusive property.

'I'm sorry,' she said quickly. 'I had forgotten. Why didn't you wake me sooner?'

His lips curled in a sneer. 'Because my dear little sister wouldn't let me. I was all for dragging you out of bed at the crack of dawn. We're not in the habit of sleeping late. Perhaps you'll remember that?'

Gisele eyed him aggressively. He certainly wasn't trying very hard this morning to maintain their truce. 'Nor am I—normally. But the combination of a long journey, Cornish air, and constant harassment must have knocked me off my feet. I'll see that it doesn't happen again.'

A grim brow lifted. 'Don't worry, *I'll* make sure. Now hurry, I don't want to make a day of it.'

A devil got into her. 'You sound as though you're not too eager to buy that ring!'

Nathaniel swore beneath his breath and the door whooshed as he pulled it savagely behind him. Gisele smiled to herself and scrambled out of bed. It delighted her to see that Nathaniel was not happy with the situation which was ironically of his own making.

CHAPTER EIGHT

THE ring was out of this world. Even Catherine could not get over it. Gisele had expected something neat and unobtrusive, not costing too much since it was a token gesture. But Nathaniel had insisted on buying an immense emerald in an antique gold setting, surrounded by tiny hand-cut diamonds.

'It's fabulous!' exclaimed Catherine when they eventually arrived home. 'I bet it cost a fortune. He must love you very much, Gisele.'

Gisele slanted Nathaniel a mischievous glance.

'It was the only one that matched her eyes,' he said offhandedly. 'I'm going for a swim, if either of you ladies want to join me?'

Gisele looked questioningly at Catherine, who laughed. 'Yes, I do swim—it's the one thing that the accident hasn't affected. Nat had the pool built specially for me. You go with Nat, Gisele, and I'll join you later. It takes me a little while to get ready.'

'Can I help?' asked Gisele quickly, marvelling anew over this woman's determination not to let her disability ruin her life.

Catherine shook her head. 'Meg will look after me. It's what she's paid for.'

And she was being paid to help Catherine in another, entirely different way! Again she hoped it wouldn't be too long before she heard some of the wonderful stories Catherine was supposed to be so good at making up. She could do with something to keep her occupied. She did not relish the thought of being Nathaniel's constant companion, even though

his sister seemed intent on pushing them together at
every possible moment.

It had been difficult in Plymouth that morning.
Nathaniel's mood had been offputting. He had not
been particularly bad-tempered, but neither had he
been very friendly. He had been coolly aloof, pleasant
enough when spoken to, but even the salesman in the
jeweller's had looked puzzled by his lack of affection
towards his supposed fiancée.

They had lunched in a pleasant restaurant and
walked across the Hoe, looking at the statue erected in
memory of Sir Francis Drake, who had played his
famous game of bowls there before setting out to
destroy the Spanish Armada.

The swimming pools and sunbathing areas built
cleverly into the rocks on the shore were humming
with holidaymakers, each and every one enjoying to
the full the glorious sunny summer weather.

Gisele had felt envious of their capacity to enjoy
themselves. Maybe she had got the most handsome
man in Plymouth by her side, but he was certainly not
much fun at this moment.

And now Catherine was suggesting they swim
together! It was harder work than she expected, trying
to convince this plucky young woman that they were
deeply and happily in love.

She went up to her room and changed into a blue
bikini that was at least three years old, but was the
only one she possessed. She had promised herself a
new one this year, but had never got around to it. If
using the pool was a regular thing, though, maybe she
ought to go out and buy a couple.

It was very brief, covering her where necessary, but
that was all. She had used it for sunbathing on the
balcony of her flat, not swimming.

Carefully she studied her reflection, wondering

what Nathaniel would think. It certainly left nothing to the imagination, emphasising the high, proud thrust of her breasts, her trim waist and long slender legs.

His tap on the door startled her, but when he pushed it open she grew angry. 'Perhaps you wouldn't mind waiting the next time? I could have been naked!'

He gave a slow smile, his eyes insolently appraising, not missing one inch of her lightly-tanned skin. 'For what little that covers it makes no difference.'

Gisele snatched up a towel and threw it about her shoulders. 'You have no right coming in!'

'I don't see why,' he said cheerfully, 'I didn't realise my—er—fiancée was afraid to let me see her beautiful body. It's even more fantastic than I imagined.

She eyed him heatedly, sluggish pulses beginning to stir. 'I am not your fiancée, and you must have seen plenty of girls in bikinis, so why make a song and dance about it?'

'Am I?' His eyes twinkled with amusement. 'It seems to me that it's you who's making the fuss. I'm quite happy.' And he looked it! Leaning indolently against the door-jamb, his arms folded, his lips curled humorously.

Gisele had been so incensed by his unexpected appearance that she had not realised he too was in swimming gear. Now she looked at his lean firm body, tanned to a deep shade of mahogany, rough hairs darkening his chest but in no way disguising its strength. Black trunks stretched across his hips, thighs powerful, calves muscled, he was undisputedly, compellingly male.

When her eyes arrived back at his face he was grinning. 'Touché now, is it? Except that I don't mind you looking at me.'

She shook her head in exasperation, deciding that his earlier controlled mood was preferable to this mocking banter. 'Let's go.' She strode forward and attempted to push past him, but he shot his arm across the doorway, effectively blocking her exit.

Gisele drew in her breath as without warning a wave of pleasure swept over her. It was unfair that he should be so strong and virile—and herself so suddenly vulnerable.

He towered above her and as she raised her eyes to his she felt dizzy. The impact of those sensual depths sent impulses dancing through her nerves, his raw masculinity sending shivers down her spine.

With an effort she dragged her eyes away, concentrating instead on a spot somewhere in the middle of his chest, watching his rhythmical breathing, feeling almost hypnotised by the steady rise and fall.

Nathaniel laughed, a low amused sound. He knew exactly the effect he was having on her. He whipped the towel away and dropped his arm on her bare shoulders, and together they walked from the room.

Gisele discovered that a tiled corridor led from the kitchen to the pool. The house extension had been built around this area so that from outside the pool was not visible at all.

The room had a glass roof and the walls and floor were tiled in aquamarine with a delightful pattern of sea-horses depicted in gold. Chairs and tables, potted plants and exotic palms gave it a Mediterranean air.

There were changing cubicles, a dryer room for towels and swimsuits, as well as a plentiful supply of clean towels—and a sauna. All very impressive. Surprisingly there was not the solarium Gisele had once imagined Nathaniel to use. She guessed his tan came from the great outdoors after all.

She stood and looked at everything for a full two minutes. 'You had this built for Catherine?'

'It was the least I could do,' he said roughly.

'Whatever my sister wants she has. She loves swimming, and it's good therapeutic exercise. Even so, I shall never make up for what I did to her.'

Gisele wished he wouldn't keep blaming himself. His sister didn't, so why should he? Yet what could she say? Time perhaps would help, certainly not anything she or even Catherine might advise.

'Let's swim,' she said brightly. 'It looks so inviting. Gosh, if I lived here I'd never be out of it!'

She thought he gave her a strange look before he dived clearly into the water, but could not be sure. For a few second she stood and watched. He was a powerful swimmer, his arms cutting effortlessly through the water, making it look ridiculously easy.

She was nowhere near his standard, and she wondered whether he would make fun of her feebler efforts. She jumped in and began a determined breast-stroke. Exactly how Nathaniel got behind her she never knew, because one moment he was at the opposite end of the pool, the next capturing her legs and pulling her down.

They surfaced together and she gasped, tossing her hair back from her face. 'Warn me the next time you decide to do that,' she laughed. 'I had the shock of my life!'

'It was intentional,' he grinned, his teeth gleaming white against his wet tanned skin, his coal-black hair moulding the shape of his head. 'I wanted to see if it would make your heart beat faster.'

Again before she had time to realise what was happening he pulled her backwards against him, his arms wrapped like tentacles about her waist, one hand beneath her breast on her heart.

His heart thudded against her back and she knew that her own echoed in response, his big firm hand accelerating it even more. He lifted his legs and swam

on his back, pulling her along with him, and it was
fortunate he held her, because her response to his vital
male body was complete.

She felt lightheaded and giddy and not at all in
control of her emotions, let alone her limbs. Nathaniel
was rendering her powerless, and the longer he held
her the weaker she grew.

He chuckled softly in her ear, a deep sensual sound,
his hands making their own exploration of her slender
weightless body.

Gisele did not have the strength to resist. It was an
extraordinary sensation, their bodies moving silkily
together, more erotic than anything she had ever
imagined.

When their feet finally touched the bottom he lifted
her into his arms. His kiss was cool and damp but
exceedingly stirring, and the masculine smell of him
filled her nostrils, sending a new havoc of sensation
flooding through her.

His mouth left hers to slide over her wet smooth
skin to her throat, to the hollow between her breasts,
and then back again to claim her mouth confidently.

Gisele had never before been made love to in a pool,
and the experience was mind-shattering, making her
dizzy with desire and excitement so that she wriggled
in his arms, uninhibitedly and unconsciously moving
herself against him, her hands beginning their own
exploration of his back and shoulders.

Nathaniel's muscles felt as though they were sheathed
in silk, rippling as he moved, his kiss deepening until
both their hearts were beating fit to burst.

Catherine's voice shattered their unconsciousness.
'Hey, you two, are you sure you want me to join you?'

Gisele jerked and struggled to escape, noting for the
first time the woman sitting on the edge of the pool.
Nathaniel laughed and held her more tightly. 'Come

in, Catherine. The water's superb!'

'As if you'd notice,' mocked his sister, sliding into the water and then doing a powerful crawl in their direction.

Gisele felt embarrassed, even though she knew Catherine had seen nothing untoward in their actions. 'Let me go!' she muttered fiercely. 'This is ridiculous!'

'There's nothing wrong in kissing my own fiancée.' Nathaniel's eyes slid in amusement over her face. 'In fact I would say it's a very pleasurable occupation.'

'You're a pig,' she accused.

'You're enjoying it,' he returned.

She would be lying if she said she wasn't, so she contented herself with a haughty glance. He laughed and let her go, moving his arms so suddenly that she dropped through the water like a stone. When she surfaced he was talking to his sister.

After that they swam up and down for a good half hour, Nathaniel organising her and Catherine into races which Catherine invariably won. And not because Gisele let her. She was a strong swimmer, completely at home in the water.

It proved, thought Gisele, what a very active person she must have been before the accident, and made it all the more difficult for Nathaniel to accept that he had not been to blame.

When he had first asked her to come down here she had thought him unduly insistent—now she could understand why he wanted to help his sister. He led such a full life himself it killed him seeing Catherine a virtual prisoner. Wouldn't it be an achievement if she managed to get her stories published, despite her handicap? And she, Gisele, would be a part of it.

Meg brought them a jug of iced orange juice and a plate of delicious home-made biscuits, and they sat at the side of the pool chatting desultorily.

Gisele was vitally aware of Nathaniel's long brown leg next to hers beneath the table, and although she could not be sure whether it was deliberate, it was nonetheless extremely disturbing.

His eyes flicked over her with wry humour and though it was warm in the pool room, with the sun's rays piercing the glass roof, she knew this was not the reason for her body heat.

And Nathaniel, damn him, knew exactly how she felt. He now knew that she found him sexually attractive, that she was beginning to thaw out, and it was giving him the utmost satisfaction to add to her torment.

More than anything she wanted to go to her room, only the thought of his sister enjoying their company restraining her. It was a relief when Catherine eventually said that she'd had enough.

'I'll tell Meg,' said Nathaniel instantly.

'No need,' exclaimed his sister. 'She'll be preparing dinner and I have all the time in the world. Just wheel my chair over, will you, then you can look after Gisele. She's your first priority now.'

His eyes swivelled to Gisele and he smiled slowly. 'Of course. How could I possibly forget?'

His mockery was not lost on her, but Catherine appeared not to notice anything wrong. 'I disturbed you once, now I'm going to leave you strictly alone until dinner-time. Take Gisele for a walk, if she has any energy left, or drive into Padstow and show her the shops.'

Nathaniel fetched Catherine's chair and helped her into it, then stood behind Gisele, resting his hands lightly on her shoulders. 'What's it to be, then? A walk, the shops? Or have you anything else in mind?'

She did not really want to go anywhere with him. She would prefer to shut herself in her room and hide away from the temptations of his devastating male body. Never would she have guessed that simply looking at him, seeing him near-naked, could arouse such earthy feelings, when she had tried her hardest to bury them. It made her cross with herself for reacting in this manner, and cross with him for being what he was.

When she did not answer his hands slid up her neck into her hair. Gisele trembled and tried to knock him away, but he caught her wrists and held them over her shoulders, straining her body backwards so that her breasts were high and taut, her nipples erect through the thin material of her bikini.

He bent low and kissed her and the male scent of him enveloped her, and there was no way she could escape. Nor, if she was totally honest with herself, did she want to. Her lips parted, accepting his kiss, and her head spun until she felt she was being transported out of this world.

Vaguely she was aware of Catherine leaving, but she did not move, nor even make any demur when his fingers slid inside her bikini top, cupping her breasts, his thumbs stroking and teasing her nipples, torturing her, until she could hold back a cry of pleasure no longer.

He groaned and moving swiftly pulled her to her feet, encompassing her in arms of steel, his hungry mouth possessing hers, drinking the sweetness he found.

There was a soaring exhilaration in the feel of his hair-roughened skin against hers, and all thoughts of resistance fled. He was kissing her deeply and hungrily as if he never wanted to stop.

Being kissed by Nathaniel was like drinking a very potent wine. He went straight to her head, bubbles of drunken excitement rising in her veins. When the effects wore off she would feel deflated, and definitely ashamed, probably angry, but at the moment she did not care.

He was kissing her as if he meant it, as though he found her more desirable than any other woman he had met. And he was by far the sexiest man she had ever come into contact with. He had to be, otherwise he would never have got through her defences.

After the Adrian affair she had been very, very careful not to let any man close. What was happening now was completely out of her control. Thoughts floated and were distorted until she felt mindless and senseless, pressing herself wantonly against him, feeling strange primitive urges and the funniest experience that someone had taken the bones out of her legs and replaced them with cotton wool.

She felt limp and delirious, and completely feminine. Nathaniel made her feel special, as though her body was driving him crazy, and there was nothing at all he could do to stop himself.

When at length with a shuddering sigh he put her from him he was trembling as much as Gisele, his face pale beneath its tan. 'I'm sorry, that wasn't part of the agreement. I'll try not to let it happen again.' He looked anguished. 'You're so damned irresistible, that's the trouble.' His eyes raked her face and he cupped it between his palms and kissed her gently.

His restraint was to be admired. He wanted her so much that his body shook—and Gisele was in a similar state herself. All her well-intentioned vows had fled. She had forgotten that she hated men, that she didn't trust them, that she wanted nothing more to do with them.

'Hold me, Nat,' she whispered, and it was like someone else speaking.

He took her into his arms and held her as though she were a fragile flower. 'So you're not the ice-maiden that everyone at Thorne & Forest said you were? I'm glad.' His voice was as husky as her own.

But his words caused some of Gisele's pleasure to fade. Her head jerked questioningly. 'Ice-maiden? What do you mean? Why should they say that?'

'Because you never let any man near you after you were jilted,' he said softly, 'until David. And I doubt if he got far. You shouldn't let one broken affair do this to you, Gisele. Every man's not the same.'

'Oh no?' With sanity came anger. 'Are you trying to tell me that *you've* not broken any hearts?'

'Not that I'm aware of,' he said levelly. 'Most of the girls I date are in a different league. They know exactly what they're doing, whereas you tempt a man quite unconsciously. You're unaware of the power in this beautiful body. It's quite a heady feeling to know I'm the first man to make you aware of yourself.'

She pulled away from him and crossed her arms quickly and defensively over her breasts. 'How do you know that? You're a bigheaded swine, and I hate you!'

He laughed. 'You'd have hated me even more if I hadn't stopped when I did, and it doesn't bear contemplating what you'd have thought of yourself. Run along and get dressed. We'll take that walk and blow the whole thing out of our systems.'

Gisele ran, simply because she could not bear to be with him any longer. How could she have behaved in such a manner? Sex for the sake of sex! It sickened her. She had never imagined that she, Gisele Latham, would respond like that to a man she did not love.

A deep and utter loathing for herself consumed her and she had no idea how she was going to face Nathaniel again. He had been amused, as well he might. It was no novelty to him, having a woman fall at his feet. The novelty was in getting through to someone reputedly ice-cold!

That was another thing: she had never realised they called her 'the ice-maiden' behind her back. Okay, she had kept men well at bay, but not because she wasn't capable of loving; simply because she was afraid of loving. She could not bear the thought of being let down a second time.

She stripped off her bikini and stood beneath the shower, and this time she really did need to wash Nathaniel Oakley out of her hair. Her body felt unclean where he had touched her, her mind too, with the shameful thoughts that had cascaded through it. She guessed she would have to live with those for the rest of her life.

When Nathaniel pushed open her door she was ready, sitting on the edge of the bed, white denims tugged over her hips, a loose cool green top covering her aching breasts. Her whole body ached—a mixture of shame and the unmerciful scrubbing she had given it.

She gave him a quick nervous glance, noting that he too wore jeans and a navy open-textured shirt, the short sleeves stretched over bulging biceps.

'Ready?' He behaved as though nothing had happened. It was difficult to believe he could push the whole thing to the back of his mind. Hadn't it meant anything to him? Or was he so used to responsive females that another one made no difference?

Compressing her lips Gisele sailed past him, her head high. A whiff of something musky reached her nostrils, making it even harder to hang on to the thin thread that held her together.

They walked towards the cliffs as though it held a fatal attraction for them both. She remembered the lamb and asked how it was—not because she wanted to talk, but something had to be said to break this dreadful silence.

'Meg let him go. I suspect he's gone back to his mother. I'll find him and cut off the plaster once his leg's had time to heal.'

They walked along the cliff-top, not too near the edge, but close enough to hear the roar of the surf and feel the occasional ocean spray in their faces.

The sky was a clear summer blue, the sea away from the shore deceptively calm. Gulls wheeled and cried above their heads, gannets and cormorants filled every nook and cranny in the cliff-face.

Nathaniel, his hands thrust into his pockets, reeled off a few names of the cliffs: 'Pepper Hole, Stack Rock, the Cat's Back, Butter Hole, Marble Cliffs.' They sounded very mysterious and exciting.

Gisele began to relax and then caught her foot in a rabbit hole. Nathaniel's arm shot out and he pulled her to him, and the agony began all over again. Although he immediately let her go the awareness was there—on both sides.

They sat down in a sheltered hollow and it was as though the world belonged to them alone. 'Has Catherine said anything to you about her writing?' Nathaniel lay back, his hands beneath his head, chewing idly on a piece of grass, but his calm manner did not deceive her.

Gisele concentrated on pulling the petals one by one off a daisy. 'Not yet, but I've not really seen very much of her.'

'I think she will before long,' he said. 'It's not something she can keep to herself. It fills her head— she has precious little else to do. I'm glad she likes you. It's a big weight off my mind.'

His eyes were closed now and it was almost as if he were talking to himself. Gisele looked at him, taking in every inch of his chiselled face, imprinting it in her mind for all time. What she could not understand was why a man such as he, the very type that she deplored, should have such an amazing affect on her.

'I like Catherine too,' she said quietly. 'I shall be honoured to help. She's a marvellous person, so courageous. I know you told me about her, but even so I didn't expect to find a woman with such a strong character.'

Nathaniel smiled, even though his eyes remained closed. 'It runs in the family, hadn't you noticed?'

'I'd have to be blind not to,' she returned lightly.

'She has my mother's looks but my father's determination. I'm my father all over again, or so I'm told. He was a good man, full of true British grit. I'm very proud of him.'

It was not difficult to imagine an older version of Nathaniel. The same harsh rugged features, compelling dark eyes that missed nothing, black hair turning grey. He would be a distinguished man, a man whom people admired.

'I think I would have liked to have met your father. Your mother must have missed him very much. Didn't she and Catherine mind staying in the house alone? It's so isolated—especially without a man to look after them.' Gisele shuddered.

'My father is still here in spirit. He was a member of the lifeboat crew, and he lost his life at sea. It was the way he would have wanted to go. And I think my mother thought it disloyal to turn her back on the sea after that. Cornishwomen are tough, disasters at sea are a part of their lives.'

Catherine was tough too! Gisele felt all of a sudden that she was unworthy of being in this house with this family. Her own troubles were trivial compared to what they had suffered.

'You make me feel very humble,' she said softly.

Nathaniel's eyes opened. 'Why should that be? You're a different breed, a different generation.'

'Catherine is my generation,' she said sadly.

'My sister is one in a million. I still can't get over her using her hands. I never thought I'd live to see it happen. I thought she'd be helpless for the rest of her life. But don't put yourself down, Gisele. I like you the way you are.' He ran the back of his fingers down her cheek. They were warm and firm and set her nerve-ends tingling.

Her eyes were drawn to his and for minutes they looked at each other, his fingers continuing their caress, each stroke sending fresh shivers down her spine.

She felt an overwhelming urge to lie down beside him and have those strong arms hold her close. Her body ached with a desperation she had not experienced in a long time.

In fact, after Adrian had let her down, she had never expected to feel this way about any man again. Indeed, she had been careful not to. Apparently she had collected the label 'ice-maiden' on the way, but even that was better than being taken advantage of.

But now a chink had appeared in her armour, and Nathaniel was doing just that—taking advantage. He had discovered she was not totally immune and was amusing himself at her expense. And she was responding!

As the horror of the situation hit her she scrambled to her feet and began running. She heard Nathaniel call and thought she heard him coming after her, but she could not be sure. And no way was she going to look back.

It was appalling to think she was following the same pattern as every other female he came into contact with. Hadn't she told Ruth and the other girls in the typing pool exactly what she thought of them for drooling over him? And now she was doing exactly the same thing!

What was it about him that appealed to her sex? He was certainly not the helpless type a girl would want to mother. He was so arrogant and masterful it was a wonder any woman fancied him. Unless they liked to be possessed, to be dominated? She certainly didn't.

Over the years she had become totally independent—and she wanted to stay that way. She did not need Nathaniel Oakley, or any other man, for that matter. She liked her life the way it was.

It had been a mistake to let him bring her here. She ought to have guessed he wouldn't be able to keep his hands off her. He was the type of man who always had to have a woman in tow. And she just happened to be convenient!

She reached the house and fled up to her room, closing the door and leaning back against it, her heart thudding, her cheeks burning. It took a few minutes for her breathing to return to normal, for the drumbeat to fade from her ears.

When it did she heard a sound like something being dragged along the floor. At first she thought it was Nathaniel, then she decided the noise did not come from his room, but somewhere further along the landing.

Opening her door, she listened again, holding her breath, suddenly realising it came from Catherine's room!

Frowning now, she made her way along the softly carpeted hall. The sounds grew louder, the dragging noise repeated at intervals. Gisele wondered what on earth was happening.

Meg must be in there, but she could hear no voices. Unless Catherine was in trouble? Perhaps she had fallen and was pulling herself along the floor? Perhaps she had called and no one had heard?

Gisele's heart raced for a very different reason this

time. Without stopping to think she turned the handle and pushed open the door. Then she stopped and her mouth fell open.

'Catherine! You're—walking!'

CHAPTER NINE

GISELE'S first thoughts were that Catherine had been fooling them. Then she saw the grim determination on her face, the lines of strain and fatigue, and knew this was for real. Nathaniel's sister was making yet another valiant effort in her battle to lead a normal life.

Catherine clung to the edge of her dressing-table and looked guilty at having been found out. 'Come in and shut the door quickly,' she said urgently.

Gisele did as she was bidden, crossing to the slim girl with the feather-light body and the face of an angel. 'I don't understand?'

'Help me to my chair,' said Catherine faintly, her chest heaving, perspiration like tiny silver jewels beading her brow.

She sat down heavily, waiting a few minutes to regain her breath. 'I didn't expect you back yet. It's my secret, Gisele. Promise you won't tell Nat?'

'Of course,' said Gisele quickly. 'But——' she frowned, puzzled, 'I thought the doctors said you would never walk again?'

'It shows what they know,' said Catherine contemptuously. 'They've never heard of the Oakley determination! I absolutely refuse to spend the rest of my life in a wheelchair. They said I'd never use my hands. I've proved them wrong there—and I'm going to prove them wrong about my legs as well.'

'And you don't want Nathaniel to know until you can walk?'

Catherine shook her head vigorously. 'I want it to be a really wonderful surprise. It crucifies him, seeing me like this. I think maybe that's why he doesn't come down very often, although he phones me every day. It will be such a weight off his mind when he sees me walking. You saw his face when he discovered I could use my hands—think what it will be like when I walk!'

It was a struggle for Gisele not to show the compassion she felt for this fine woman. 'He'll be delighted. Why don't you tell him now?'

'Because it's hell,' admitted Catherine. 'If he sees me sweating blood it would finish him. I sometimes ask myself whether it's worth it. Then I think of Nat, and picture his expression when he sees me on my feet.' She smiled sweetly. 'It's all I want out of life, Gisele, to make Nat happy. No man should suffer like he does because of what he thinks he's done. He's such a good, kind man, and I think you're the luckiest girl in the world to be marrying him.'

Gisele felt her colour rise and was convinced she must look guilty. But she could not spoil Catherine's enthusiasm at this moment by admitting it was a pretence. It would destroy her pleasure in their happiness, it might even make her give up trying to walk.

'He's rather special himself,' she said, knowing Catherine would interpret her wrongly.

'He's wonderful,' agreed the other girl. 'He's done so much for me. Every girl should have a brother like Nat. Have you a brother, Gisele?'

'I'm an only child,' she admitted, her heart suddenly racing as through the window she caught sight of Nathaniel striding towards the house. There was something about the set of his shoulders that suggested he was not pleased. 'And my parents are dead, so——'

'So you're lucky to have Nat look after you,' finished Catherine delightedly. 'He'll do that all right.

He'll protect and cosset you and probably spoil you. You won't have to worry about anything again for the rest of your life. How I wish I could find a man like Nat to look after me!'

It was the first hint she had given that her disability in any way got her down, and as if she already regretted what she had said, she added quickly, 'Here he is now. Go to him, Gisele, before he comes up and sees me like this.'

And although she had no desire to talk with him again Gisele left the room and went downstairs. His sister was still flushed from her exertions. He would certainly want to know what she had been doing.

She met him in the hall. He frowned, brows knitting angrily, the contours of his face looking harsher, more clearly defined, the lines scored from nose to mouth deeper. 'Why?' he demanded fiercely.

'Why what?' she asked pertly, needing time to think.

'God damn you, you know what I mean! Why did you run away?'

'Did I? You must be imagining things.'

His fingers bit aggressively into her shoulders. 'Something happened. One moment you were responding to me, the next staring as though I had two heads.'

Pain shot through her and she tried to push him away. 'You could well have!' she cried angrily when she found it impossible to escape. 'There are two sides to your character—the charming seducer, who always gets the woman he wants, and the cold-hearted bastard who callously cuts them out of his life one he's finished with them!'

His eyes narrowed until they were no more than two glittering slits, nostrils flaring above a mouth that was grimmer and tighter than she could ever remember. 'And you think that's what I intend doing to you?'

Gisele lifted her chin and stared at him coldly. 'I don't think it, I know it.'

'Considering the short time you've known me, you're hardly in a position to make such a statement,' he snapped.

'Aren't I? Gisele felt herself burn with rage. 'It's as clear as the nose on your face. And you're right, I was responding. All I can say is, thank God I came to my senses in time!'

She looked at him hostilely, hardly feeling the pain now. 'You're very clever, I'll admit that. You almost had me fooled. When you said you liked me I actually believed you—just for a second. Isn't that hilarious?'

'It slays me,' he said, contempt in his voice. 'But who do you think you're trying to kid? Certainly not me. It's yourself you're afraid of. I've cracked your ice and you're afraid I might discover the woman beneath. Tell me, Gisele, exactly who are you keeping yourself for?'

She snapped her lids disdainfully. 'Not you, that's a fact. Let me go!'

Nathaniel grinned, but the humour was malicious, and his grip tightened. 'But you enjoy teasing me? Perhaps it was a calculated gamble, letting me catch a glimpse of the hot-blooded woman you really are? But when you realised it was your fingers that would get burnt and not mine, you got scared and ran?'

Gisele's cheeks flamed. It was near enough to the truth to let her know he was nobody's fool. 'You think what you want!' she snapped furiously.

'I think I ought to teach you a lesson.' His hands slid from her shoulders to the small of her back, pulling her inexorably against him. 'No one plays with fire without getting burnt. Hasn't anyone ever told you that, my lovely Gisele?'

As he moulded her insistently against him she felt as

though she was burning already. His fierce body heat made a mockery of the clothes that separated them. It was as if their two naked bodies were fusing together. Wave after wave of sheer desire throbbed through her, and she could no more have ignored him than she could cut off her own hand.

It was sheer insanity, letting him do this, but the matter had been decided for her. There was nothing at all she could do about it. Her mind warred, but her body instinctively responded.

Her hands moved freely to slide beneath his tee-shirt and explore the firm smooth back beneath her sensitive fingertips, arching herself against him convulsively, her lips parting eagerly under his.

He crushed her to him like a man demented, searching her mouth hungrily, his lips demanding, bruising, utterly ruthless. When he swung her up into his arms and began to mount the stairs she felt she ought to struggle. Indeed she made a weak attempt to free herself, but the effort was too much. She was putty in his hands.

And then the strident ring of the telephone disrupted them. Nathaniel's steps faltered, but he carried on up. Gisele was not sure whether she felt relief or disappointment. Perhaps a mixture of both?

They heard Meg's hurried footsteps across the hall, then her pleasant Cornish voice. 'Nathaniel, it's Morwenna!'

He frowned harshly, his eyes jagging into Gisele like a machete blade. With an angry exclamation he dropped her to her feet. 'I'll be back,' he warned. 'I've not finished with you yet.'

But that brief respite brought Gisele to her senses. Whoever Morwenna might be she was thankful for her. She went to her room and for the first time since coming to Stormhaven turned the key.

Not until then did she realise how her limbs were trembling. To think that she had been in danger of losing her pride and maybe her virginity—to a man like Nathaniel Oakley! It did not bear thinking about. She must be insane!

Yet even as she thought this her whole body throbbed with desire, and she knew there was a very big danger of this whole thing happening all over again.

Responding to Nathaniel was the worst thing she could do. It made her close her eyes to all that was wise and sensible. Each time she saw him now it would be the same; there would be no escaping the feelings that flared.

She really ought to return to London before things got out of hand, but how could she let Catherine down? Catherine already saw her brother as a broken man. If his supposed fiancée ran out on him it would, in Catherine's eyes, be the last straw.

Surely if his sister could be brave and make a determined effort to pretend there was nothing wrong, then so could she. It would not be for long. Two weeks, he had said, then he would go back. While she, Gisele, would remain here with Catherine. Twelve more days! If they went as slowly as these last two it would be purgatory.

Ten minutes later she heard him bounding up the stairs. She held her breath as she waited for his hand on the knob, then she heard Catherine asking who was on the phone.

She opened the door and the two of them were outside. Catherine had changed for dinner and looked as calm and beautiful as ever. Nathaniel looked out of sorts and flicked Gisele a caustic glance before answering.

'It was Morwenna. She'd heard I was here and has invited herself to dinner.'

'How nice!' exclaimed Catherine. 'But she might have given us more notice. Have you told Meg?'

He nodded tersely.

'Then you'd best get changed,' said his sister. 'Knowing Morwenna, she'll be here before we've had time to breathe!'

He looked again at Gisele, tight impatience on his face, angry because his plans had been thwarted. Misinterpreting his glance, Catherine laughed. 'She's not likely to run away, Nat!'

'Isn't she?' he snarled, then because his sister gave him an anxious look, 'It's all happened so quickly I sometimes can't believe it.'

'I think the best thing you can do, Gisele,' chuckled the girl from her chair, 'is marry him as soon as possible and put him out of his misery. I've never seen him so edgy!'

Gisele did not know what to say. She looked at Nathaniel over the top of his sister's head, her green eyes anxious, but he did not help. He merely stared at her coldly before lifting his broad shoulders and moving into his own room.

Catherine said swiftly, 'I've done it again. I'm sorry—I should learn to mind my own business.'

'It doesn't matter,' said Gisele, smiling weakly and going back inside. She closed the door and stood for a moment trying to decide whether it would be best if she left without completing her mission.

It had to be either her or Nathaniel. They couldn't both remain, it wasn't fair on Catherine. Already the girl sensed that there was something not quite as it should be between them.

Perhaps having Morwenna here this evening would help? Except that she felt a stab of jealousy over this unknown woman. She was evidently well know, but who was she? A relative, or an old flame of

Nathaniel's? There was no reason why she should think this—except feminine intuition!

She dressed carefully, just in case, in a peacock blue dress shot through with silver and various shades of green. She fixed her hair up, adding a defensive armour of eyeshadow and mascara until her eyes were the focal point in her face.

When she eventually made her way downstairs Morwenna had arrived. Gisele heard her voice before she entered the room, high-pitched and confident, contrasting strongly with Catherine's husky charm and Nathaniel's sensual growl.

'Engaged? To whom? Why didn't I know?' She did not sound too pleased. And if she fancied Nathaniel herself there was every reason for her to be angry; it must have come as a terrible shock.

Gisele steeled herself and made her way inside. All eyes turned in her direction. Gisele was not sure who got the biggest jolt, herself or Morwenna.

There was no doubt who the girl was. That shining brown hair and sultry dark eyes could belong to no other than the girl Nathaniel had accompanied to the concert, who had spent more time looking at him than at the musicians themselves.

Nathaniel performed his part well. He moved at once, taking her arm, kissing her cheek, and no one other than Gisele knew there was no warmth in it, that his kiss was perfunctory and nothing more. 'Gisele, my sweet, come and meet Morwenna.'

It was an effort to walk across the room, and she knew that the dark girl had no interest in being introduced to her either. They were both aware that Nathaniel was the only reason they had been forced together.

'Gisele, Morwenna Tremain. She lives in Padstow, so you'll probably see quite a lot of her while you're down here. Morwenna, this is Gisele Latham.'

The two girls touched hands. Morwenna's was icy cold and she withdrew quickly, as though contact with Nathaniel's fiancée was abhorrent. 'Isn't all this a bit sudden?' she asked coolly. 'Didn't I see you at a concert in London a week or so ago—with another man?'

Gisele smiled frostily, hating Morwenna on sight. She was typical of the sort of woman she expected Nathaniel to associate with—pretty but brittle, full of herself and caring little about anyone else. Except Nathaniel!

Morwenna took his arm possessively, not letting it bother her that he was engaged to another woman. 'Darling, don't you care? Doesn't it matter that Gisele has other man-friends?'

He smiled and patted the hand that held his arm. 'That was before we were engaged. What Gisele did then was up to her. Now she's not so free.'

'You mean she's under your control?' A delicate shudder ran through Morwenna. 'What wouldn't I give to have a big strong man like you telling me what to do!'

Gisele felt nauseated. Why was it that women thought Nathaniel was the epitome of what a man should be? Couldn't they see any further than the end of their noses? Didn't they realise his charm was superficial?

She accepted the sherry Nathaniel handed her, sipping it as she watched the dark girl talking to him. Not once did Morwenna take her eyes off his face. 'Why didn't you tell me you planned to come down? We could have travelled together. It's so boring, driving all this way alone.'

'I didn't know when I last saw you,' he said.

'Neither did you tell me that things between you and—that woman—were serious. I thought you hardly knew her. Doesn't she *work* for you?' She made it sound like a dirty word.

Nathaniel smiled. 'She's my secretary.'

The slanting dark eyes rested hostilely on Gisele before switching back to her partner. 'And I suppose now that you've got yourself engaged you'll have no time for poor little me?'

Gisele felt a gnawing in the pit of her stomach, flaring upwards until she could hardly breathe. Surely she wasn't jealous? Not of Morwenna? Nathaniel was welcome to her; they were eminently suited.

'I'll always have time for you, Morwenna, you should know that.'

Nathaniel's reply made her wince. How could he? In front of Catherine, as well! She glanced at his sister, who sat quietly in her chair, her drink in her hand. The flamboyant Morwenna in her red skin-tight dress outshadowed the pale, fair girl—not that Catherine looked unduly worried.

A smile curved her lips and her eyes were soft as they rested on her handsome brother. She really did idolise him, thought Gisele. He did no wrong in her eyes. Even giving his attention to someone other than his fiancée did not seem to bother her.

Perhaps it was because they had known Morwenna for a long time? Or perhaps she thought the other girl posed no threat?

It did not look that way to Gisele. Morwenna resented her, that was clear. It had upset her to learn that Nathaniel was engaged. There was no doubt that she saw herself as the future Mrs Nathaniel Oakley.

And she, Gisele, went oddly cold inside at the thought that Morwenna might have lain in his arms. It was a foolish reaction, considering she hated him, no doubt brought about by the very strong physical feelings she had experienced earlier.

She crossed to Catherine and tried to pretend there was nothing wrong. 'I expect it's nice to have company. You must find it frightfully lonely?'

'Lonely?' echoed Catherine. 'Cornwall is my heart and soul. I sit at my window and watch the sea. Occasionally Meg takes me out on to the headland. The scenery is always changing—I adore it. I'd be lost in London. All those people! I couldn't stand it.'

'But in the winter, surely then you wish you were nearer civilisation?'

Catherine smiled and shook her head. 'We keep well stocked with food and logs. Even if we're snowed in we can keep warm and eat. I can't imagine ever living anywhere else. And I have my thoughts to keep me company. Sometimes I—ah, here's Meg. Aren't you simply starving? I know I am!'

Gisele wondered whether Catherine had been about to confide—and felt a moment's disappointment. She so wanted to justify being here.

They took their places at the table, Morwenna next to Nathaniel, Gisele opposite him beside Catherine. 'You're very lucky,' said Catherine with a wicked smile to her brother as Meg placed melon and orange cocktails in front of them. 'Three ladies to entertain—a blonde, a brunette and a redhead. You couldn't have arranged it better had you tried!'

He smiled at her before his eyes flickered across to Gisele. 'I'm indeed honoured. I think I must have the three most beautiful women in the world.' Then he turned to Morwenna, and it was upon her that his eyes rested longest.

It was plain which one he favoured, even though it was she, Gisele, who wore his ring. She twiddled it now, eyeing him scornfully, wondering how he could do this to his sister.

Maybe he did like Morwenna best, but for the

moment surely he should be concentrating his attention on herself? How was she to play her part if he ignored her?

He made several attempts during the meal to draw her into the conversation, and because of Catherine she made an effort, but each time Morwenna changed the topic, talking about people whose names meant nothing at all.

In the end she sat silently toying with her food, wondering if she could possibly say she had a headache and go to bed. They took their coffee into Catherine's sitting room, Morwenna pulling Nathaniel down on to the couch, leaving Gisele to take the chair next to Catherine.

And because she thought it would be unfair on her hostess to leave her with the other two, Gisele stayed, sipping her coffee, watching Nathaniel and Morwenna chatting animatedly. An inexplicable twinge of pain ran through her each time the attractive brunette touched his arm, her blood-red nails pointed and wicked, or whispered something in his ear.

'They're such good friends, those two,' said Catherine. 'I'm so glad, because Morwenna's not like me, she hates it down here.'

'Then why does she stay?' asked Gisele sharply, wondering how his sister could possibly condone their friendship when he was supposed to be engaged.

'She helps run the hotel, or should I say she more or less runs it herself these days. She's a very busy lady.'

But not so busy that she could not find time to spend with Nathaniel. And as for running a hotel—it somehow did not fit in with the image Morwenna projected. Maybe she did her job well—she looked reasonably intelligent—but she would be a figurehead only; she was not the type to welcome her guests herself.

Holidaymakers liked the personal approach, they liked to feel that they were being welcomed as members of one big family. Anyone seeing Morwenna would be chilled by her haughtiness, her over-sophistication, which was more suited to London than the seaport of Padstow.

Her oval brown eyes never left Nathaniel's face, and her high brittle laugh grated on Gisele's nerves. In the end she could stand it no longer. She got to her feet. 'If you'll excuse me, I'll say goodnight.'

Nathaniel directed her a chilling glance, but he dutifully came across and pecked her cheek. If that was the best he could manage, thought Gisele tightly, he needn't have bothered!

Morwenna said goodnight with an effort, and Catherine asked why she was going so early.

'I have a headache,' she said, and it was true. It was no longer an excuse, her head felt as though a steel band was slowly being tightened around it, making her eyes ache and her body numb.

Nathaniel had no right doing this to her. She was supposed to be his fiancée, and as such it should have been herself he devoted his attention to this evening, not the beautiful Morwenna.

That the dark girl was his type there was no doubt, and she had possibly been a welcome diversion, but need he have made it quite so clear? It was acutely embarrassing.

She tossed and turned, unconsciously listening for Mowenna to go. She heard Catherine's lift as it came up the stairs, and then the soft swish of her electric wheelchair as it passed her door. But the elegant Morwenna remained.

It was well past midnight when she eventually heard movements in the hall, the girl's high-heeled sandals clicking on the marble tiles, the door opening and closing—then silence! Had they left together?

Unable to contain her curiosity, Gisele pushed back the sheets and crossed to the window. She had left her curtains open so was able to look down into the courtyard without anyone seeing a telltale movement.

There was only one car in sight—Nathaniel's! And even as she looked the engine purred into life and his headlights cut an arc into the blackness of the Cornish night.

Morwenna must have come by taxi—no doubt with the express purpose of getting Nathaniel to take her home. There was a chair near the window, and Gisele sat down and tried to analyse her feelings where Nathaniel was concerned.

There was a physical attraction, yes, but she was not on her own in that respect. Most women swooned over him—he was that type of man. But seeing him with Morwenna had brought totally new and different feelings rushing to the surface. She had scoffed at the thought that she might be jealous—but was it really all that far from the truth?

And if she was jealous, what did it mean? Was she in danger of falling in love with Nathaniel? *No!* She shook her head violently. That could never be. She had no intention of falling in love with any man again.

Adrian had spoilt her in that respect. She had fallen head over heels in love with him, too blind to see that he did not love her in return. But she did know that Nathaniel did not love her, so whatever these feelings, they had to be kept strictly under control.

The trouble was, Nathaniel was not altogether the callous man she had first thought. He cared about his sister to such an extent that the fact that he had committed her to a lifetime in a wheelchair sometimes drove him crazy.

He could never forgive himself for causing his mother's death. He quite openly loved and admired his courageous father. He thought more of a lamb's safety than his own.

These things counted for far more than the fact that he had a track record a mile long where women were concerned. It was a man's nature to hunt the opposite sex, just as women like Morwenna Tremain dressed to attract them. The brunette certainly made no secret of the fact that she found Nathaniel a sexually exciting man.

So far as she, Gisele, was concerned, he had brought her here to do a job, and until it materialised he found it entertaining to break through her barriers. That was as much as she meant to him. He probably thought the term 'ice-maiden' for a hot-tempered redhead highly unlikely, and because there was nothing else to do concentrated his attention on battering down her defences.

He had done that all right—her heart raced alarmingly now every time she saw him. But forewarned was forearmed, so the saying went. It was simply a matter of keeping a tighter rein on her feelings. She knew exactly where she stood with him, all she had to do was make sure he had no opportunity to get through to her.

The drive into Padstow should have taken no more than a few minutes, yet it was over an hour before he returned. All that time Gisele sat staring out of her window across the blackness of the heath and the still silent sea beyond. If it hadn't been for the stars that carpeted the sky like a network of diamonds there would have been no telling where the sea ended and the sky began.

It was an effort to drag herself back into bed. Her limbs were stiff with sitting for so long in one position, her head throbbed as if someone pounded it with a sledgehammer, and her heart felt unusually heavy.

She heard Nathaniel come in, the door close and bolts being shot, then his soft footfalls as he mounted the stairs and walked along the landing. Perhaps now she would sleep?

But when he stopped outside her door and the knob squeaked, oh so slightly, as he turned it, she sat bolt upright, fixing her wide eyes on the black space that widened to reveal his shadowy bulk.

Once inside he gently closed the door. 'I thought I might find you awake. I'm glad you haven't forgotten we have some unfinished business to attend to.'

He walked towards the bed, unbuttoning his shirt as he did so.

CHAPTER TEN

GISELE could not believe Nathaniel was serious. She reached out and snapped on the bedside light, blinking as it dazzled her eyes, then glaring furiously. 'Get out! There's nothing that you and I have to say!'

He smiled sardonically. 'Who's talking about words?'

Gisele's heart thudded and she was acutely conscious of her semi-naked state beneath the covers. Her fingers tightened on the edge of the sheet.

He stepped closer, dark eyes gleaming in his harsh face. There was a hint of steel in the thrust of his jaw, and an arrogance in the proud tilt of his head. His open shirt exposed the wide muscled chest above dark trousers that clung to and emphasised narrow hips and powerful thighs.

But even stronger than all this was his aura of virility, masculine aggression at its peak, a ruthlessness which suggested that whenever Nathaniel Oakley wanted anything he pursued his course relentlessly. And at this moment he wanted her!

'Nathaniel, no!' Gisele pressed herself back against the pillows as he towered menacingly above her, the sheer primitive maleness of him making her breathless.

His eyes flicked her face mercilessly, noting the apprehension, her trembling lips and the pulse that flickered rapidly at the base of her slender throat.

'Nathaniel, no,' he mocked. 'That isn't what you were saying earlier. When I carried you in my arms you were mine to do with as I liked. Can you deny it?'

Her eyes searched his face for one trace of understanding, but there was nothing except rugged determination. 'Would you believe me if I did?'

He shook his head savagely and one big hand snatched back the sheets before she had time to stop him. 'You had your fun with me,' he snarled, 'now it's my turn. No woman makes a fool of me, Gisele—you'd best remember that.'

'I didn't, I wasn't——' she cried frantically, her eyes almost filling her face. 'Nat, you don't understand!'

'Nor have I any wish to,' he snarled, ripping off his shirt and throwing himself on the bed beside her.

Nathaniel in this mood frightened her, even though her body responded alarmingly and shamelessly to his masculinity.

One arm was flung heavily across her waist, pinning her brutally, a taut thigh pressed against the softness of her own, and when his mouth sought hers she felt tears well.

Her response to him, though, was total. Emotions like quicksilver raced through her limbs, bringing her achingly, throbbingly alive.

But bearing in mind her recent good intentions she struggled with every ounce of strength, pummelling with her fists, twisting her head from side to side in an endeavour to avoid his hungry mouth, finally sinking her teeth into his shoulder and rejoicing when she felt the salt taste of blood.

'Stop fighting me, damn you!' he grated roughly. 'You want this as much as I do.' His hard hands caught her head, forcing it back against the pillow, while he closed his hot mouth on hers.

This is the beginning of the end, Gisele thought, as a shudder wrenched through her, and she lay still, tensing herself for his assault on her senses.

It was as sweet as she knew it would be. The touch of his lips, the warmth of his hands, melted her fragile defences; and although she was determined not to reveal the depth of her arousal, there was no way she could quench the fire that leapt through each and every nerve until her whole body was aflame.

One hand left her cheek to roughly pull her flimsy nightie down over her shoulders and cup the fullness of a breast. Gisele cried out and arched herself involuntarily against him.

A tremor ran through Nathaniel and his mouth left her lips to trace a scorching line down her throat. He lifted his head and allowed his eyes to make a thorough appraisal of her breasts before with a groan he took an erect nipple into his mouth.

Gisele no longer thought of fighting, she gave herself up to the ecstasy of Nathaniel's lovemaking, knotting her fingers into his thick strong hair, holding his head to her breast, an anguish of longing sweeping over her.

When he claimed her mouth yet again his eyes were glazed with a desire that matched her own. 'God, I want you so much,' he muttered thickly, urgently, the hammer-beat of his heart against her chest adding credulity to his words. 'Tell me you want me as well!'

He sounded as though it was desperately important to him that she feel the same way, that he had given up all thoughts of teaching her a lesson and wanted only to satiate his desire.

But it was not easy for Gisele to admit her feelings. Want him she did, quite desperately. But it went against every principle to give in to Nat now. She closed her eyes, refusing to look at him, fighting the waves of passion that flooded through her.

'Gisele, my love, admit it.' His palms cupped her face, his eyes burning into her, by their very intensity forcing her lids open. 'You want me as much as I want you.'

She looked at him and tried to shake her head. His face was all pain and angles, ravaged by a depth of emotion that racked him as deeply as it did her.

'*Gisele!*' he implored, taking her mouth again, erotically running the tip of his tongue over her lips before plundering the soft moistness within. He was gentle now, persuasive, intent on drawing the response he so badly wanted.

And this very tenderness made Gisele ache for him all the more. She needed him to be strong, to bruise her with his body, to assert his male dominance. She cried out and wrapped her arms and legs round him, feeling the sudden tightening of his muscles and the swift intake of breath.

'Oh, Nat!' she breathed hoarsely. Yet even when her whole body cried out, when she knew that only he could assuage this pain in her loins, she still found it impossible to put her feelings into words.

'My love, my sweet love, do you want me to love you?'

She nodded, her soft lips parted and swollen from his assault, her green eyes luminous and never leaving his face.

'Then tell me, Gisele, let me hear you say it,' he said huskily.

'I can't,' she whispered, suffering agonies.

'It shouldn't be hard,' he groaned. 'I want you, Gisele, I freely admit that.'

His eyes were locked into hers, and such was his compulsion that Gisele swallowed the last of her guilt. She moistened her lips and said painfully, 'Nat—please—make love to me.'

She could actually feel tears as the request was forced from her, but once she had said it, once she had admitted the depth of her feelings, she felt a glorious spread of warmth, a relaxing of her defences.

Tomorrow she would regret it, but for the moment her need of Nathaniel was all that mattered. Their bodies craved each other, hunger throbbing urgently through their veins.

Her eyes glowed as she looked into his face and there was a corresponding warmth in his. Then, as if something inside his brain snapped, shutters slammed down over them and he pushed himself away.

'Nat?' Gisele was puzzled, reaching out to him, feeling suddenly cold and bereft. 'What's the matter? I've said what you wanted. Isn't that enough? What more do you ask?'

His harsh laugh was like a whiplash and she flinched, recoiling from the cold contempt in his eyes. 'Goodnight, Gisele,' he grated. 'I never realised that teaching you a lesson would make me feel so good!'

She stared in disbelief as he closed the door. There had been no doubt in her mind that he was sincere, that what had begun as a deliberate attempt to arouse her had turned into something far more serious.

He had been as worked up as she, she knew that, and to discover it was nothing more than a ploy to get her reluctant request to make love was something she found difficult to stomach.

Yet it was true. She folded her arms across her chest and rolled on the bed in agony. He was a devious, cunning, unfeeling swine! Tears welled and spilled down her cheeks. She clenched her fists and pounded the bed. But it did not make her feel any better.

How could he do this to her? How dared he! Oh, God, how she hated him. Why had she been so naïve as to believe he felt a genuine need?

It was clear now that he could turn his feelings on and off like a tap. He was an expert where women were concerned, using them shamelessly, and tonight she had been his target. He had succeeded more beautifully than he could possibly have imagined.

Shame mingled with burning anger. She bounced out of bed and took a shower, icy cold, quelling instantly what vestige of passion remained. She towelled herself dry and dragged on a clean nightdress, climbing back between the sheets on legs that were distinctly shaky.

She could not remain here any longer to be humiliated by Nathaniel. Catherine's needs could not be helped. Tomorrow she would definitely leave. She would insist that he take her back to London, and his sister could make of it what she liked.

But when she went downstairs the next morning Catherine told her that Nat had left the house early to take Morwenna into Exeter. 'Have you still got your headache?' she asked, noting Gisele's pale face and shadowed eyes.

Gisele nodded, even though it was her heart that ached more than her head. 'I hardly slept. I think perhaps I'll take a walk. I don't want any breakfast.'

'Have some aspirin first.' Catherine delved into her bag. 'And a cup of tea at least. I wonder what's caused it. Do you suffer from migraine?'

'No,' said Gisele, shrugging. 'It's one of those things, I suppose. How long will Nathaniel be, did he say?' It seemed as though he had deliberately thwarted her plans.

Catherine poured two cups carefully, concentrating on her task before saying, 'I've no idea. Knowing Morwenna she'll keep him out all day. She does so love having Nathaniel home.'

'It's hardly fair on you,' snapped Gisele.

'I can't expect him to hang around me all the time,' said Catherine wryly. 'You know how he feels, seeing me in this chair. But it's wrong that he left you behind, and it was a teeny bit selfish of Morwenna not to include you in her invitation, though not surprising. She was very shocked to discover Nat was engaged—she considers him her private property when he's here. You mustn't mind Morwenna.'

Morwenna was welcome to him, thought Gisele nastily. She obviously knew the type of man he was and it made no difference. They were each as artificial as the other.

She took her tablets and as soon as she could comfortably excuse herself left the house. The headland held no attraction this morning. Instead she turned and walked towards Padstow, deciding she might as well have a look at the town before returning to London.

Following a rough track past the Coastguard lookout station, she went steeply downhill for quite a way, the Camel Estuary nothing more than a wide sweep of golden sand left exposed by the tide, broken only by narrow rivulets of shimmering water. It was impossible for a ship to make her passage up the estuary until the tide came in.

She came across a row of old coastguards' houses and a disused lifeboat station, and reflected on Nathaniel's father, who had lost his life for this worthy cause. Then deliberately she pushed all thoughts of Nathaniel and Catherine from her mind. It had been a mistake to become involved with this family.

It was a longer walk than she expected, following the path along the coastline, but the bracing air cleared her head and the different sights and sounds took her mind off Nathaniel.

When Padstow came into view her steps quickened and she soon became a part of the lively harbour scene. Holidaymakers jostled and smiled, semi-naked bodies soaked up the sun, children laughed and dogs barked.

Nathaniel's description of a town huddling in the shelter of the cliffs, with narrow crooked streets full of interesting shops, was an accurate one.

Old stone houses seemed to grow out of the cliff-face itself, in danger of falling into the harbour a few feet below. There was a mad jumble of artists' studios and gift shops, of cafés and boutiques.

Gisele spent an hour watching an artist depict a typical harbour scene of yesteryear, painstakingly drawing endless lines of rigging on tall-masted ships, repeating their reflection in the waters below.

Another hour was spent in a bookshop on the Strand. It was filled from floor to ceiling in glorious disarray. As well as new books and paperbacks there were secondhand and antiquarian books on almost every subject under the sun. Books about Cornwall, maps, prints. It was a fascinating shop and Gisele could have stayed there all day, except that she was afraid Catherine might worry if she did not return soon.

It was with reluctance that she tore herself away from Padstow, from the boats bobbing in the harbour now that the tide was coming in, from the lobster and crab tanks where shellfish could be chosen live and cooked to order, from the Morris dancers who suddenly appeared and set everyone's toes tapping with their cheerul music.

By the time she arrived back at Stormhaven it was late afternoon and Nathaniel had returned. His brow was black as he met her outside, his jaw rigid. 'Where the devil have you been?' he demanded.

Gisele's chin lifted stormily. 'Does it matter?'

'Of course it damn well matters,' he said strongly. 'Catherine said you'd gone for a walk, but that was hours ago. You could have fallen over the cliff—anything.'

'I've no doubt you'd have been glad to see the back of me,' she returned testily. 'I'll apologise to your sister if I've worried her, but you can go to hell.'

She tugged off the ring and thrust it at him savagely. 'This absolves all your responsibilities. If I choose to throw myself off the cliffs now it will have nothing to do with you.'

'For God's sake don't be ridiculous!' he snarled angrily. 'Do you want to ruin everything?'

'It's a stupid idea, if you ask me.' Her green eyes glinted as brightly as the sea that was a backdrop to their argument. 'Catherine's not mentioned her writing once. I'm not so sure you weren't lying, that for some devious reason you used it as a con to get me here.'

Such as last night, she could have added, but didn't. That little scene was far too raw and painful to be dragged into the open so soon. But it was typical of the type of man he was. What a fool she had been to believe he was serious about her!

He eyed her coldly. 'You've hardly given yourself time to win Catherine's confidence.'

'And there will be no more time,' Gisele said flatly. 'I want to go back to London. If you won't take me I'll catch a train.'

She received a chilling stare in response to her statement. 'Get inside, and don't talk nonsense,' Nathaniel snapped.

'It's not nonsense, I'm quite serious.' Gisele held her head high. 'Catherine has shown no sign of needing me, and I can't possibly remain here with you a day longer.'

'You have no say in the matter.' His voice was soft but authoritative. 'You stay until I say you return. I'm not having my sister upset.'

'But it doesn't matter how I feel?' Her wide eyes

rested resentfully on his face. 'I have to put up with the ignominy of you manhandling me whenever it takes your fancy. Is that the real reason you brought me here? Were you shooting me a line when you mentioned Catherine's stories? It was time to pay her a dutiful visit, but you couldn't stand the thought of being here without a woman. A pity you hadn't realised Morwenna would be available, then you wouldn't have had to bother about me.'

His eyes narrowed dangerously, piercing her thin armour so that suddenly she felt strangely vulnerable and knew she could not defy him for much longer. 'Morwenna bothers you, does she?'

Gisele arched her fine brows with what she hoped was the right degree of incredulity. 'Why should she? If you want to go to bed with her, that's all right.'

He would never know how difficult it was to say that. Her body still responded to him, even after the way he had treated her, and she could not look him in the eye.

A firm finger lifted her chin and at his touch an involuntary shiver ran through her. 'Are you denying that you're jealous of Morwenna?'

She looked at him for a brief agonising second before lowering her lids. 'I'm not jealous,' she said tightly, ignoring the emotion that ravaged her. Nathaniel's ring still lay in her palm, and again she thrust it at him. 'Perhaps you ought to give this to her? I'm sure she'd be much happier wearing it than me.'

He caught her wrist and jammed the ring back on her finger. 'It stays there!' he ground harshly. 'Now I suggest you get into the house and put Catherine out of her misery.'

Gisele tossed her head, her windswept hair catching the sun, framing her face like burning fire. 'If I know your sister she's already seen me through the window—and she'll probably also have seen me giving you back your ring. What do you think she'll make of that?'

Their eyes met and held for a brief dangerous second. 'A lovers' tiff, nothing more. She knows I'm angry because you stayed out so long. Don't worry about Catherine, I can see to her.'

'Of course,' she flung at him carelessly, 'I'd forgotten you're an expert when it comes to women. What does it feel like to come up against one who isn't so easily misled?' But who was hurt all the same.

'Don't make the mistake of thinking I don't know how to handle you.' Nathaniel took her arm and half pushed her towards the door. 'Meeting a woman with spirit merely makes it more interesting.' He grinned unexpectedly. 'Remember that the next time you feel like arguing!'

Gisele snatched free and flounced ahead. Why did he always make her feel the loser? Why couldn't someone put him in his place for once?

He left her at the door to Catherine's sitting room, but his chuckle followed her as she entered, and it took every ounce of willpower not to let his sister see that she was outraged.

Before dinner that evening Gisele decided to use the pool. It had been quite a day one way and another and a lazy swim was just what she needed. She asked Catherine to join her, but discovered she had already been in that morning, and once a day was quite enough, thank you.

The water was heavenly, soothing her verbally battered body like nothing else could. Despite what Nathaniel had said his sister was not unduly alarmed over her absence. Catherine guessed she had gone into Padstow. It was Nathaniel himself who had been concerned. 'Which is natural,' Catherine had smiled, 'since he loves you.'

Love! It was doubtful if he knew the meaning of the word. He loved his sister, certainly, but that was a different kind of love. The love between a man and a woman who planned to marry was something special; unselfish, totally consuming—and nothing at all like any of the feelings he experienced.

How did Morwenna find him? Gisele wondered. Or was Morwenna so blinded by her slavish adoration that she could see no further than the shell of the man, not realising that beneath lay a heart packed in ice? Men like Nathaniel lusted for women, but they never loved them.

She swam up and down relentlessly, her thoughts rarely off Nathaniel, trying to speculate how long he would keep her here. Eventually she decided enough was enough and hauled herself out—only to find the man of her thoughts confronting her.

'Don't go,' he said, 'join me. It's no fun swimming alone.'

Her heart leapt at the sight of his copper-tanned body, so tall and straight and essentially masculine, so virile. 'Perhaps not to you,' she managed, 'but I quite enjoy it.'

His dark eyes skimmed the curve of her breast above the blue strip of bikini, and too late she wished she had bought another in Padstow that was not quite so revealing. Except that then she had thought she was going home.

She drew in a swift ragged breath and swung away, but he caught her wrist and said grimly, 'I don't take kindly to having my invitations ignored. I want you to swim with me.'

'You're hurting!' She met his eyes hostilely, noting how relentless they had become, and shivered. They were both frightening and exciting at the same time.

Nathaniel always had his own way—and her defiance merely made him all the more determined.

Surprisingly, though, he let her go. But her triumph was shortlived when the next second a strong arm curved round her back, another beneath her knees, and she was lifted effortlessly and thrown without ceremony into the water. And it all happened so quickly that she had no time to struggle. She merely yelled as she sailed through the air, hearing his bark of laughter before she hit the surface.

When she had blinked the water from her eyes he was beside her, grinning wickedly. 'Some women never learn! Come on, let's race, let's get rid of that fire in your veins.'

The challenge was more then Gisele could resist, but she was no match for Nathaniel, as he well knew. There was satisfaction, though, in pitting herself against him, and by the time he called a halt she had forgotten her animosity and actually responded with a friendly smile.

'I should have known I was fighting a losing battle,' she panted. 'You swim like a fish!'

'You're not too bad,' he returned, placing an arm on either side of her so that she was pinned against the edge of the pool, 'for a mere woman.'

Her head jerked, as he had known it would, eyes flashing, lips parted. A cool wet mouth slid over hers, brushing aside her protest, proceeding to move to the hollow between her throat and shoulder, pressing damp kisses to her skin, so that by the time he had finished she was shaking.

'You're quite something, you know that?' There was laughter in his dark eyes. 'A real sexy little kitten once you shake off your inhibitions.'

'And that amuses you, does it?' she whipped. 'I'm afraid I don't find it quite so funny. If you must know, I think you're despicable!'

She tried to slide beneath his arms, but somehow his legs got in the way, one taut thigh pushed firmly between hers, an ankle hooked around her calf, pulling her inexorably against him.

'That's not true,' he said, his lips lifting at the corners. 'It's simply that you've never met anyone quite like me before, and no one's sure of themselves when they're walking on strange ground.'

'Hostile territory is more the term I'd use,' she finished, wishing the feel of his thigh wouldn't send waves of eroticism flooding through her. He had no right doing this!

His eyes widened. 'I'm not hostile, far from it. In fact I'm by far the friendliest native you're ever likely to meet.'

'Don't I know it!' Gisele raised her eyes heavenwards. 'Have you a list of all the girls you've smooth-talked into thinking they're in love with you?'

'We're not discussing what may or may not have happened to me,' he said firmly. 'We're talking about you. You're all uptight because of that goddamn man who needs his head examining. You're not giving yourself a chance, Gisele. You're one hell of a woman beneath that cool exterior. Am I to be permitted no more than an occasional glimpse?'

She wished he would let her go. Each tiny movement sent fresh currents through her, and the sight of powerful muscles rippling beneath the bronzed satin skin was enough to drug her senses.

'I don't understand you,' she sighed. 'Why is it so important? Aren't you satisfied with Morwenna?' She had not meant to bring the other girl into the conversation, but now she waited with bated breath for his answer.

Nathaniel's eyes gleamed with sudden brilliance. 'Why the interest?'

She lifted her shoulders, her cold wet hair brushing them so that she shivered. 'You seem to get on so well I thought maybe you were going to marry her.'

He frowned, then smiled. 'And you don't think Morwenna is my type?'

She looked at him insolently. 'I think you're two of a kind. If you marry her you should live happily unfaithful ever after.'

'And you, young lady, deserve to be punished,' he grated, his smile fading abruptly.

'For what? For speaking the truth?' Gisele lifted her chin belligerently. 'Are you trying to tell me that one day you'll settle down and get married and never chase another girl?'

'Is that so unlikely?' he returned hoarsely.

'All I know is that leopards never change their spots. I'm getting cold. Would you mind letting me go?'

'When I'm good and ready.' He slid his hands beneath her hair, knotting it between his fingers, making her his prisoner.

His breath was cool and fresh on her cheek, his over-brilliant eyes defying her to look away. 'What makes you so sure I wouldn't make some woman a good husband, when your own experience of men is so limited? When you've wrapped yourself in cotton wool to protect you from so-called wolves like me? Don't you think my experience makes me a far more likely candidate for marriage than a withdrawn little virgin like yourself?' His voice grew harsher. 'I know what life is all about, Gisele. I've lived, and loved, and lost. I've learned by my experiences. You might do as well to take a leaf out of my book.'

'And what would that make me?' she demanded. 'A harlot? No, thanks, I prefer to go on as I am.' It was far better to sail through life alone than become hurt and unhappy with a whole string of affairs. She was not that type of girl.

'It's a hard life for a woman,' he muttered against her mouth, 'without a man.'

He was not actually kissing her, yet the touch of his lips was as explosive as if he was making passionate love. His body and mouth were drugging her, each movement calculated to send rivers of sensation rippling through her.

His lips slid imperceptibly over her, his thumbs sensuously circled the delicate area behind her ears. Her heart drummed and her pulses raced all out of time with themselves.

'I could be that man,' he suggested softly, insistently.

Gisele went rigid, her eyes snapping wide to study his face. He sounded different, quite sincere. It was almost as if he were offering her marriage! The real thing!

Then all too quickly she realised this was the last proposition he would make. An affair was more in keeping. He was merely changing tactics.

Without stopping to think she lifted her hand and it made a very satisfying sound as she slapped his face. 'That's what I think of your offer!'

CHAPTER ELEVEN

NATHANIEL drew in a sharp breath, a muscle working furiously each side of his jaw. 'I wouldn't advise you to do that again.'

'And I wouldn't advise you to insult me!' Gisele grated, lips tight, her beautiful eyes sparkling.

She half expected him to hit her back, but with a harsh exclamation he swung away, hauling himself out of the pool in one swift lithe movement.

He was deeply angry, that was for sure, and she ought to be glad. Instead she felt saddened that it had come to this. Had he really thought she would be interested in an affair? Hadn't it yet sunk in how she felt about men like him?

Clumsily she climbed out herself. Her limbs shook treacherously and it was an effort to put one foot after the other. She fetched a towel from the supply kept in readiness and wrapping it defensively about her shoulders made her way to her room, mentally crossing her fingers that she would not bump into Nathaniel.

Once safely locked inside she heard him next door opening and shutting drawers. He sounded in one hell of a temper, and she wondered whether she dared venture down to dinner later. Catherine would certainly want to know what was wrong. Maybe Nathaniel could put on a face, but she certainly couldn't.

Despite the warm day Gisele was so cold she could not keep a limb still, and after drying herself thoroughly she slid between the sheets, curling into a ball and closing her eyes. It was impossible, though, to erase from her mind's eye Nathaniel's face when he had suggested he be the man in her life. What a good actor he was! He had almost fooled her.

How sincere he had sounded—and yet all he wanted from her was a little light entertainment while he was down here. Morwenna did not satisfy him—he wanted her as well!

She grew warm beneath the covers, and gradually some of her anger subsided and she fell asleep, aware of nothing until a loud banging penetrated her unconsciousness.

'Dinner!' called Nathaniel sharply, thumping her door yet again. 'It's no use trying to hide. You can't shut yourself in there for ever.'

'I don't intend to,' answered Gisele, her voice sluggish. 'I was asleep.' A glance at her watch told her it was well past their normal time for dinner. 'Tell Catherine I'm sorry. I'll be down in five minutes.'

He said nothing else, but his footsteps were loud and heavy, unlike his normal animal-like tread. He was still angry! How many women, she wondered, had had the temerity to hit him? Maybe plenty had felt like it, but none had the nerve. Or had they never refused him anything?

She pulled on a blue cotton sundress with shoelace straps. Not bothering with make-up, she tugged a brush through her hair and let herself out of the room.

Catherine, looking as charming as ever in a beige and brown spotted dress, smiled warmly. 'Hello, sleepyhead. I guess the walk tired you out more than you thought. It's our Cornish air. People say they could sleep a week when they come down here.'

Nathaniel said nothing, his back towards them, ostentatiously looking out of the window. He did not fool Gisele, but she wondered whether his sister guessed at the tension between them. Then he turned, as though suddenly aware of her presence. 'So you've decided to grace us with your presence after all?'

'Gisele can't help it if she fell asleep,' laughed Catherine. 'Stop behaving like a bear with a sore head, Nat, just because you've been kept waiting!'

He scowled blackly and his sister laughed again. 'He's always like this, Gisele, when he's hungry. You'll have to watch it when you're married—feed him on time unless you want a sharp taste of his tongue!'

Gisele smiled weakly, wishing Catherine wouldn't constantly make these references to their marriage. It was acutely embarrassing, especially with Nathaniel glowering. Anyone less lover-like was difficult to imagine. It was fortunate Catherine assumed his dark mood was due to hunger.

The meal was an uncomfortable occasion and Gisele felt relieved when it was over. Nathaniel immediately disappeared, and she sat with Catherine until bedtime, watching a programme on television that interested them both, and later listening to records.

Neither mentioned Nathaniel, though Gisele sensed his sister casting her a few speculative glances, and the next morning Catherine announced that he had gone to London on urgent business.

It was a relief not to have him around, even though she felt oddly hurt that he had not said goodbye. She swam in the pool with Catherine, gave her encouragement when she took a few painful steps, and wondered whether she dared bring up the subject of her writing. With Nathaniel no longer here she felt like an imposter.

'I think soon,' said Catherine, 'I'll show Nathaniel what I can do. It might cheer him up. He's so depressed I can only think it's because of me.'

Gisele felt a painful attack of conscience and was tempted to confide that she was the reason for his moods, but she felt it would be unfair to add to this courageous girl's burden.

A few days later she went into Catherine's sitting room to find her staring trance-like at the ceiling. She sat down quietly and watched, wondering whether she ought to snap her out of it, whether this business with Nathaniel was telling on her more than she would admit.

Then suddenly Catherine smiled. 'Gisele! I didn't see you come in. I've had this splendid idea for a novel, and I was just working it out in my mind.'

She sighed heavily and looked down at her hands. 'I wish I could grip a pen well enough to write. It's so infuriating!'

Here was the opportunity Gisele had been waiting for. Her heart quickened and she opened her mouth to make the offer. Then she closed it again just as swiftly. What would be the point? Once she got involved it would mean remaining here for goodness knows how long. There would be inevitable visits from Nathaniel; he would probably renew his attack on her defences. How could she stand it?

It would be far better to say nothing, go back to London, and then leave her job. That way she would never see him again. It was unlikely they would bump into each other. She could move to the other side of the city and their paths need never cross.

Uncannily, as though following her line of thought, Catherine continued, 'Nat's always telling me how good my stories are. He said I would have no difficulty in getting them published if I could find someone to write them down for me. I've tried a tape-recorder, but it's not the same. You do shorthand, don't you? Nat's told me how efficient you are. I could talk to you without feeling shy. Would you help me, Gisele? Would you?'

Gisele did not know what to say. On the one hand she did not want to let Catherine down, but on the other she had her own life to consider. Committing herself to Catherine now could be committing herself to months of unhappiness. What she must ask herself was whether it was worth it.

Eventually Catherine would be able to do these things for herself. Nathaniel did not realise what progress his sister was making. When he had asked her, Gisele, to do this for him, he had resigned himself to Catherine spending the rest of her life in a wheelchair, totally dependent on other people. Now it was conceivable that in the not too distant future she would be able to write her thoughts down for herself. Would it really matter if she had to wait a little while longer?

Seeing the hesitation on Gisele's face, Catherine said quickly, 'I'm sorry. You're here on holiday, you don't want to work. I shouldn't have asked. Forget I said anything.'

Gisele felt awful. 'Catherine, I——'

But Catherine cut her off. 'No, Gisele. Please, forget it.'

'But I——'

'I mean it. I shouldn't have mentioned it. You don't want to be involved in my dreary tales. They're probably nonsense anyway. Nat's biased because he's my brother.'

There was the same fierce Oakley determination on her face as Gisele often saw on Nathaniel's. Too late she wished she had not hesitated, that she had immediately and willingly agreed to do as Catherine asked.

It was useless continuing the argument now, but

tomorrow she would bring up the subject again and insist that she be allowed to help. Catherine was such an unselfish person, how could she, Gisele, possibly allow thoughts of her own unhappiness to take precedence?

She was so ashamed of herself it was difficult to act naturally after that, although Catherine was as lighthearted and happy as ever she was, making Gisele feel doubly uncomfortable.

Nathaniel returned later that same day, and Gisele left him to talk to his sister while she changed for dinner. He did not look particularly pleased to see her, and she was glad to keep out of his way.

She dressed carefully, not to impress him, but to boost her flagging morale. The dress was new, cream and silky, low-necked, sleeveless, faithfully following the lines of her body.

With extra care she applied her make-up and fastened a slim gold chain round her neck and gold hoops in her ears, knotting her wayward hair tightly and severely on the top of her head.

She looked cool and elegant, she decided, surveying her reflection critically; not exactly how she felt, but it was outward appearances that counted.

Then her door was pushed unceremoniously open and Nathaniel hurled himself into the room. 'How dare you insult my sister!' His face was flushed and ugly, the long line of his jaw rigid, his eyes black and implacable. 'Get out of this house,' he said thickly. 'Pack your bags and go. I've already called a taxi—it will be here in five minutes.'

Gisele stared at him, her brow creased, eyes wide with shock, her heart hammering. What had she done that was so awful?

'Don't look at me like a petrified owl!' he snarled, his arms swinging at his sides, fingers curled. He dragged a suitcase from the top of one wardrobe and began snatching dresses off hangers and ramming them in.

Gisele watched in fascinated horror, racking her brains for a reason behind his irrational behaviour, and could only assume it had something to do with her conversation with Catherine earlier. But Catherine hadn't been upset; in fact she had done the apologising.

'Nat,' she began persuasively, 'suppose you tell me what this is all about?'

'*Tell you!*' he snarled, whipping round to face her. 'As if you don't bloody well know! Catherine made light of it, naturally, it's not in her nature to run anyone down. But it was easy to read between the lines.' His face was white now, all angles, bones jutting from beneath his skin, eyes glazed as if in acute agony.

'Not content with insulting me by flinging my offer of marriage back in my face, you now refuse to help Catherine write her book. That's just about the most cruel thing you could have done, Gisele, and I hope to God you'll have it on your conscience for the rest of your life!'

Her mouth fell open and her heart sank to the bottom of her stomach. She stared at him, feeling the colour drain from her face until it felt as taut and stiff as a cardboard mask.

She forgot Catherine, she forgot everything, except that her first thought had been right. He had meant marriage! And she had slapped his face. She had told him where to get off. It was no wonder he had reacted as he had.

'Oh, God!' she managed shakily, perhaps even more shocked that he had proposed than by her reaction to it. It did not make sense. Nothing was making sense any longer.

'Oh, God, indeed!' he snapped icily. 'I suppose you're going to tell me now that it hadn't occurred to you exactly how much damage your cold-hearted refusal could do?'

'To you?' she whispered huskily. 'Nat, I didn't——'

'To Catherine, damn you,' he interjected harshly. 'She is the reason you're here, in case you've forgotten. It's the first time she's mentioned her ideas to you, and *you*——' he paused, breathing heavily, nostrils flared, lips tight, '*you* take it into your own hands to *refuse!*' He was rocking now on the balls of his feet, eyes rimmed with red in his white face.

'It wasn't like that, Nat,' she protested. 'I——'

'I don't want to hear your excuses,' he snapped furiously. 'The damage has been done. Get packing!'

He flung another case at her and she opened drawers and pushed things in, but all the time she looked at him, wondering how she could make him listen, what she could say that would put things right between them.

Her actions were slow and he lost patience, knocking her to one side, grabbing handfuls of undies and cramming them into corners.

'Please listen, Nat,' she implored, wringing her hands, swallowing a dry lump in her throat. 'Let me explain. Catherine——'

He turned on her savagely, his eyes burning with rage and contempt. 'Shut up and get the rest of your things together! I wish I'd never brought you here. What is it you've got against Catherine, for pity's sake? Or did you do it simply to get back at me? Was that it, eh?' He paused for breath. 'It was a hell of a shock to discover I'd been taken for a ride, but never did I think you'd hurt my sister. I ought to kill you!'

Gisele drew in a sharp painful breath, blinking away tears that scalded the backs of her eyes. She shook her head. 'I don't know what you're talking about?'

'Don't give me that!' He smashed a fist into the palm of his hand, and Gisele reeled as if he had struck her.

'What do you mean, taken for a ride?' she whispered faintly. Her eyes were deep shimmering pools of pain, her brow puzzled.

He glared coldly. 'Mandy should learn to be discreet. I heard a whisper, but no one was prepared to talk—except Mandy. The poor girl was in quite a dither when the big sexy boss took time to say a few words to her.'

Gisele's cheeks flamed and she clapped her hands to her face in horror. There was only one thing he could be talking about—that stupid dare! He thought she had led him on and then, to use Ruth's own words, dropped him. But that was certainly not the reason she had slapped his face. She had never dreamt he was serious. It had been a most unusual proposal.

His black brows lifted and disappeared into the thatch of hair that fell angrily across his forehead. 'You remember!' he accused drily. 'What a convenient memory you have! But that's not the point at issue. I can take care of myself. I'm more concerned with what you've done to my sister.'

Gisele shook her head repeatedly, her face creased in anguish, her body deathly cold. 'No, Nat, *no*! I didn't do it deliberately. I thought——'

'You can think all you like,' he barked, 'the damage is done. But exactly why did you refuse to help Catherine?'

'I didn't refuse, I—I——' She searched for words that he couldn't twist. 'I——'

'Took so long in answering that it was perfectly clear you didn't want to do it, but hadn't the nerve to say so. Hell——' Again his fist pounded his palm, and Gisele cringed, her whole body shaking.

'Why won't you listen?' she cried, the tears now

racing hotly down her cheeks. 'Why won't you give me a chance?'

'Do you deserve one?' he sneered, his lip curling, eyes condemning. 'I don't think so. I've heard enough to convince me that you're nothing but a sham. You're rotten through and through, and if I ever set eyes on you again—I'm warning you—I won't be responsible for my actions!'

He waved clawed fingers before her eyes, his body stiffened with rage, his harsh chiselled face distorted. 'It's only because of Catherine that I'm keeping my hands off you now,' he finished.

Gisele shuddered and backed, the blood pounding in her head. She thought she was going to faint. Nathaniel had always been a dangerous man, but in this treacherous mood he was lethal.

And too late—she realised that she loved him. Why hadn't she guessed it before? The feelings that she had thought were purely physical were a new love dawning. She had so thoroughly conditioned herself after the Adrian affair that she had not been able to see what was happening to her.

She realised now that what she had felt for Adrian was not love at all—at least not love of the same depth and quality as she felt for Nathaniel. She had told herself that men were not to be trusted, she had put them all in the same class as James and Adrian. But it was simply not true.

Nathaniel liked girls, he had had plenty of affairs, and never made any secret of the fact. So far as he was concerned it was an essential, healthy part of life. But basically he was a good kind man, and there was no doubt in her mind now that he would be a faithful husband. And had she not been so determined to see only bad in him, she could be his wife! This was what hurt most of all.

Her own stupidity, her own blindness, her conviction that he was not a type to be trusted, had all served against her.

For a few seconds she stared at him, her breast heaving as she fought for control, then, galvanised into action, she began feverishly throwing bottles and brushes into her bag, shoes into a holdall, all the time casting scared glances over her shoulder, convinced that at any moment Nathaniel would lose his last thread of sanity. There was no point in trying to make him listen, not now. She had lost whatever chance she had had.

When at length everything was packed she faced him. 'I'm ready,' she whispered, her heart bleeding, feeling as though she was beginning to die.

He eyed her coldly, and for one last time she held his gaze. His face was contorted with an emotion stronger than himself, twisted beyond all recognition.

Those eyes which could make her melt with desire were burning with hatred. His hands, which could stimulate and excite, were curved stiffly, fingers locked into position. His whole body rejected her, made her feel like the scum of the earth. And oh, God, she loved him!

When he jerked into life and picked up her cases she jumped. Then the door opened—and Catherine walked in!

Only Gisele knew how much it must have cost to hold herself straight and give no outward show of pain. She had seen Catherine's stumbling steps, the agony of moving limbs that had been still and useless for so long.

Yet there was no sign on her face that the effort was too much. She walked stiffly and slowly, yet purposefully, towards her brother, her eyes on him alone.

Gisele held her breath, afraid to make a sound to

break the silence in that room. Nathaniel still gripped the cases, but the ravaged lines of pain had faded. Instead he stared at his sister, his mouth hanging open. He too had stopped breathing.

Catherine had almost reached him when her legs began to weaken. She took a step and faltered. Nathaniel dropped the cases and caught her as she fell, swinging her up into his arms and carrying her to a chair near the window.

He knelt in front of her and took her hands into his, Gisele for the moment forgotten. He was trembling uncontrollably, shaking his head, his eyes locked into those of his sister.

'It's a miracle! It's a bloody miracle!' And then they were both crying and laughing, and he wrapped her in his arms and murmured her name over and over again.

Gisele cried too. It was a very moving moment, one that really she ought not to have witnessed. She was on the verge of leaving the room when a horn honked loudly outside and she knew that the taxi had arrived.

Nathaniel stiffened and pushed himself up, but his voice was tender when he spoke to Catherine. 'I won't be long. Gisele's leaving, she needs a hand with her cases.'

'*No!*' exclaimed Catherine, loud and strong. 'No, Nat. She stays!'

His head jerked. 'You don't understand. I'll explain later.'

His sister lifted her chin, a glint of the Oakley stubbornness in her eyes. 'There's no need, Nat—I was listening. I think it's Gisele who should be given the chance to explain.'

'Gisele?' he echoed incredulously, treating Gisele to another of his contemptuous stares. 'I brought her into this house in good faith. What she has done to you I shall never forgive.'

'Gisele has done nothing to me,' said Catherine softly. 'I have no quarrel with her, although from what I heard I gained the impression you didn't bring her purely and simply to introduce her as your fiancée.'

A muscle worked spasmodically in his jaw as he looked from one to the other, obviously wondering how much he should say. Then the taxi-driver sounded his horn impatiently.

'I think you ought to tell him there's been a change of plan,' said his sister sweetly. 'And I'll talk to Gisele while you're gone.'

Nathaniel glared furiously. 'I shan't be long.' He strode out of the room and they heard him hurry along the landing and leap down the stairs two or three at a time.

'Sit down,' said Catherine, smiling gently, 'before you fall down. You look all in. I heard some of what my brother has put you through, but not all. Perhaps you'd like to tell me?'

Gisele shook her head. 'There won't be time. He'll be back before I've begun.'

'Only if you insist on arguing. Come on, let's hear it.'

So Gisele sat on the edge of the bed, her fingers twisting nervously in her lap. 'It's quite a long story, but basically Nat wanted me to help you with your writing, except that he didn't think you'd open up to someone who was here specifically for that purpose. He said you fought shy of anyone but relatives—hence the false engagement. He wanted you and me to be friends first. I was to wait for the right moment to offer my help.'

Catherine's delicate brows lifted, her blue eyes wide; yet her lips curved, showing that she was also amused at the elaborate plan that had been conceived on her behalf. 'So why the hesitation when the moment came?'

Gisele lowered her eyes. 'I'm sorry about that, Catherine, I really am. I felt awful about it, you've no idea, but something happened between Nat and me and I didn't want to commit myself to staying here.

'I'd already decided to go back to London and throw in my job when you asked if I'd help.' She looked at Catherine sorrowfully. 'I was torn—but in the end my conscience won, and I was going to tell you tomorrow that I'd do it.'

'But Nat put his oar in first?' suggested Catherine ruefully.

Gisele nodded. 'I feel as though I've been physically flogged, and I can't see what talking about it will do. I can't stay here, not now.'

'What happened to make you so bitter?' asked the other girl. 'I knew there was something wrong between you, but I had no idea what, and I didn't think it was my place to interfere.'

'I'm not sure I should tell you,' said Gisele wryly. 'He might not like it.'

'Who cares what Nat likes?' said his sister rudely. 'You can't leave me in suspense!'

Gisele sighed. 'Nat proposed, and I didn't realise it was a proposal—I thought it was a—an unhealthy proposition, so I slapped his face.'

Catherine chuckled, 'That I would like to have seen!'

'It doesn't finish there, though,' said Gisele sadly. 'I was engaged once, and then jilted on my wedding day. It made me very bitter towards men. One of the girls at work dared me to get Nat to fall for me and then ditch him as a sort of beautiful revenge on the male sex in general.

'I never seriously considered it, even though I'd heard Nat's reputation as a lady-killer—and he was the type of man I hated most. But now Nat's heard about this bet and he thinks I rejected him deliberately.'

'And you didn't? In fact you didn't realise he had proposed? That sounds typical of Nat. What are your feelings for him?'

Gisele smiled uneasily. 'Would you believe me if I said I've just discovered that I love him? It hit me like a ton of bricks when he told me to go. I knew I felt some sort of response to him, but I never realised it was love. I didn't want to fall in love—it only brings heartache. And I've just given myself the biggest dose imaginable!' she finished ruefully.

'You could try telling him you love him,' suggested Catherine. 'I'm quite sure he loves you. I've seen the way he looks, as though you're the most precious thing in his whole life.'

Gisele put her hands over her face. 'Oh, Catherine, if only it were that easy! But you're mistaken. Perhaps he did love me, or thought he did when he proposed, but not any longer. You should have seen the way he looked at me just now. I think he wanted to kill me!'

She did not hear Nathaniel come into the room or see Catherine put her finger to her lips.

'He'll come round,' said Catherine softly.

A shudder ran through Gisele. 'I don't think so. He really hates me now. I wish he had killed me. I thought he was going to, he was so angry. I really wish he had. I don't think I can go on, Catherine. I——' She lifted her head—and saw Nathaniel!

His face was gaunt and white and he stared at her as if seeing her for the first time. Her eyes flashed from him to Catherine. 'Why didn't you stop me?' she asked faintly. 'Why didn't you tell me he was here?' The words were hardly audible from her bloodless lips.

'Gisele,' he breathed hoarsely, then dropped heavily on the bed beside her, crushing her in his arms. 'Oh, Gisele, what have I done to you?'

She closed her eyes and buried her head in his chest

and let his strength flow into her. It was a long time before her shivering stopped, before she found the power to lift her face and look at him.

He had aged in the last few minutes; deep lines scored from nose to mouth, his sensual lips drawn down at the corners, eyes deep black pits of agony, skin ashen, drawn tightly across his chiselled bones.

'I love you, Gisele—I thought you knew. I'm so sorry. I——'

She worked a hand up between them and placed her fingers gently over his lips. 'Shh, Nat, don't blame yourself. We were both mixed up. I didn't know you cared—I thought you desired me, yes, but I had no idea you loved me.'

'With every breath in my body,' he said huskily. 'From the moment you walked into my office and flashed those green eyes and tossed that red hair I knew I was hooked. I knew you were the one woman I'd been waiting for.'

His kiss was infinitely sweeter and far more satisfying than any of the others. This was the first kiss given in true love. It was a sealing bond, promising a lifetime of happiness.

'Perhaps, Nat, you'd fetch my chair?' Catherine's gentle voice reached them as they surfaced for air. 'Then you can carry on in private this business of getting to know one another.'

Momentarily Gisele had forgotten his sister. Now she beamed across at her. 'Catherine, thank you.' There was no need for anything else. They understood each other perfectly.

'You needn't go,' said Nat gruffly. 'If it wasn't for you, my dear sister, I'd have lost the only woman I've ever truly loved.'

'I really think you should be alone,' insisted Catherine. 'If you won't fetch my chair then I'll walk—though I'm not so sure I can make it again today.'

He fetched the wheelchair quickly and helped her into it, then stood looking down, raking a hand through his hair. 'Why didn't you tell me? It's so marvellous, after all this time. Oh, lord, so much is happening all at once. I think I'm going to be a very happy man!'

Catherine smiled secretly and left, and he closed the door behind her. Gisele rose and walked unsteadily into his arms. 'Nat, it's not only a miracle Catherine walking, it's a miracle you loving me. Is it really true?'

'As true as I'm standing here,' he said. 'I'll never shout at you again, Gisele, not as long as I live. Didn't you truly realise I was asking you to marry me that day at the pool?'

'I thought you were after an affair,' she returned shakily. 'It's the strangest proposal I've ever heard! We weren't even particularly friendly at the time.'

His grip on her tightened. 'We weren't very friendly most of the time. When did you decide not to carry on with that foolish bet?'

'I never went along with it,' she said firmly. 'I had no intention of getting involved with you. I knew I was the one who would end up getting hurt. I've hidden my vulnerability under a cloak of independence for a long time now. And I was glad of it when you started amusing yourself at my expense. But gradually, without my even realising it, you crept under my skin. I didn't know I was falling in love, though, not until you told me to go.' It had been the worst moment of her life.

Nathaniel looked both angry and sad at the same time. 'That guy who jilted you really did a great job. You're so mixed up. I wish I could get my hands on him! Did you truly love him?'

Gisele lifted her shoulders. 'I thought I did.' Except that it was nothing like the feelings she had for this tender giant of a man. 'But it was a whirlwind affair and I never really got to know him. It turned out he was using me to make his girl jealous. She'd walked out on him, you see, and once he'd got her back I was ditched. It's as simple as that.'

'He left it a bit late,' he snorted angrily. 'And when I asked you to pose as my fiancée you thought I was using you too?'

She nodded.

'Poor Gisele—but it wasn't like that at all.'

'So why did you send for me in the first place?' she puzzled.

He smiled wryly. 'Curiosity. I'd heard stories about you and wondered how a girl with your colour hair could be so frigid. I wanted to see for myself this beauty they termed "the ice-maiden", little knowing I was going to fall immediately and irrevocably in love.'

'So you had no plans then to turn me into your secretary, or bring me down here to help Catherine?'

'I was looking for a new secretary,' he said, 'but the idea of asking you to help Catherine didn't dawn on me until I'd worked with you for a while. It suddenly struck me that Catherine would love you the same as I did—and you'd already proved you were capable of working under pressure. It seemed an ideal solution.'

Gisele dimpled shyly. 'It's ironic that it all fitted in with Ruth's ridiculous dare. And I'm sorry I didn't trust you. I've always been too afraid to fall in love again.'

Nathaniel kissed her, his mouth hungry for love, seeking each curve of her face, throat and ears, his arms binding her to him, crushing her mercilessly. She felt her own desire flare and clung to him shamelessly now, pressing her body close, never wanting to let him go.

'Gisele, Gisele.' He put her from him roughly, shaking his head and moving away. 'If we carry on like this I won't be responsible for what happens. I stopped once—do you remember? It was the hardest thing I've ever done, and I'm sorry if I hurt you. But I don't think I'd have the strength to do it again.'

'I don't mind. If we're going to be married—and I presume that is the idea—' she smiled impishly, 'it won't make any difference.' But she loved him all the more for his restraint.

'I want to get married today,' he said. 'Tomorrow. Hell, how much notice do you have to give? We shall get married at St Petroc's, of course. And I suppose we'll have to invite our various relatives, or they'll never forgive us.'

'I have no family,' Gisele said quietly.

He looked serious all of a sudden. 'I wondered why you never mentioned your parents. I thought perhaps you didn't get on with them. What happened?' His tone was gentle.

'My father died of a heart attack when I was twelve. My mother remarried a man who turned from a super guy into a bastard who treated her so badly she took her own life,' said Gisele quietly.

Nathaniel closed his eyes and his frame shook. He came to her and took her hands. 'Gisele, I had no idea, I'm so sorry. It must have been ghastly for you. No wonder you hate men! I thought it was just that boy who'd done it to you. I thought you were being overly dramatic, but I now see there was far more to it. I'm sorry.'

'It doesn't matter.' She shook her head. 'I'm over it now—and at least I don't think *you'll* change. I've seen all the different sides of your character—and I still love you.'

He groaned hoarsely. 'And I love you. Remember that day on the cliff when you nearly fell over? God, I never want to live through anything like that again! If I'd lost you I think I'd have thrown myself down as well.'

'How do you think I felt,' queried Gisele, 'seeing you? I didn't know then that I loved you, but I certainly have never been so scared in all my life. You didn't do my heart much good.'

'I reckon we've both given each other a few shocks,' he smiled, 'but it's the future that concerns us now. We're going to be very, very happy, I know.'

Gisele drew in a breath and asked a question that had been bothering her for the last few minutes. 'Where does Morwenna fit into all this? I don't think she took our engagement seriously. At least, it didn't stop her from fawning all over you. She won't spoil things for us?'

'Morwenna?' Nathaniel asked sceptically. 'Why should she?'

'She loves you!' What a stupid question.

'Like a brother,' he laughed. 'She's our cousin—didn't Catherine tell you? Although I must admit, I did attempt to make you jealous. She runs the hotel with my aunt and uncle. Lord, we've been together since we were kids. She's familiar with me, but that's the way she is. We're just very good friends. If she doesn't give us her blessing I'll want to know why.'

'But she didn't seem to like me,' frowned Gisele.

'That's because she doesn't think any woman is good enough for her handsome cousin. If she had her way she'd pick my wife for me. Oh no, my love, Morwenna is no threat.'

'Then I've nothing else to worry about.' She sighed contentedly, moving her soft feminine body into the circle of his arms.

Nathaniel gathered her close and groaned. 'Catherine's miraculous recovery, and you, my passionate beauty, for my wife. What more could a man ask? I really must be the luckiest person in the world.'

'Not so lucky as me,' she smiled. 'I have you.'

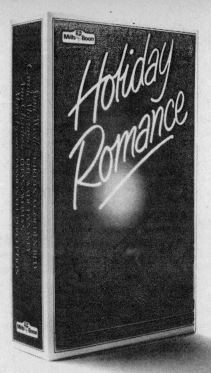

To be read with caution whilst sunbathing.

The Mills & Boon Holiday Pack contains four specially selected romances from some of our top authors and can be extremely difficult to put down.

But take care, because long hours under the summer sun, engrossed in hot passi can amount to a lot of sunbu.

So the next time you filling your suitcase with t all-important Mills & Bo Holiday Pack, take an ex bottle of After Sun Lotion.

Just in case.

PRICE £4.40 AVAILABLE FROM JUNE 1986

Mills & Boon

Take 4
Exciting Books
Absolutely
FREE

Love, romance, intrigue... all are captured for you by Mills & Boon's top-selling authors. By becoming a regular reader of Mills & Boon's Romances you can enjoy 6 superb new titles every month plus a whole range of special benefits: your very own personal membership card, a free monthly newsletter packed with recipes, competitions, exclusive book offers and a monthly guide to the stars, plus extra bargain offers and big cash savings.

AND an Introductory FREE GIFT for YOU.
Turn over the page for details.

As a special introduction we will send you four exciting Mills & Boon Romances Free and without obligation when you complete and return this coupon.

At the same time we will reserve a subscription to Mills & Boon Reader Service for you. Every month, you will receive 6 of the very latest novels by leading Romantic Fiction authors, delivered direct to your door. You don't pay extra for delivery — postage and packing is always completely Free. There is no obligation or commitment — you can cancel your subscription at any time.

You have nothing to lose and a whole world of romance to gain.

Just fill in and post the coupon today to MILLS & BOON READER SERVICE, FREEPOST, P.O. BOX 236, CROYDON, SURREY CR9 9EL.

Please Note:- READERS IN SOUTH AFRICA write to Independent Book Services P.T.Y., Postbag X3010, Randburg 2125, S. Africa